"THE WASHER'S OVERLOADED. QUICK, HIT THE stop button," Jill shouted struggling to remain standing amid a cascade of suds.

"Missed." Drew said as she grabbed him around the waist. They both went down, clinging to each other. Landing on his side, he curled his arm around her to break her fall. Hip to hip, chest to breasts, they couldn't have been closer unless they were both naked.

Once she caught her breath, she began a slippery struggle to put space between them, but the harder she tried to disentangle herself from his embrace, the more her pelvis did a bump and grind against his hip.

"Let me help you or you'll slip again," he warned.

"I've got to turn this off," she said, but only made it up on one knee before sliding on top of him. Her face was inches from his and bright red. Pushing frantically off him again, she nearly made it to her feet, but slipped, landing astride his hips. Soap suds dripped from one ear. "Drew, do you have any idea how this looks?" she whispered desperately .

"Like Deborah Kerr and Burt Lancaster on the beach?"

"Drew!"

"You're right," he said, twisting her onto her back and locking his knee over hers. "I think Burt was on top." He looked at her for a long moment, then took her mouth in a breath-stealing kiss. . . .

WHAT ARE *LOVESWEPT* ROMANCES?

They are stories of true romance and touching emotion. We believe those two very important ingredients are constants in our highly sensual and very believable stories in the LOVESWEPT *line. Our goal is to give you, the reader, stories of consistently high quality that may sometimes make you laugh, sometimes make you cry, but are always fresh and creative and contain many delightful surprises within their pages.*

Most romance fans read an enormous number of books. Those they truly love, they keep. Others may be traded with friends and soon forgotten. We hope that each LOVESWEPT *romance will be a treasure—a "keeper." We will always try to publish*

LOVE STORIES YOU'LL NEVER FORGET
BY AUTHORS YOU'LL ALWAYS REMEMBER

The Editors

LOOKS
LIKE LOVE

SUSAN
CONNELL

BANTAM BOOKS
NEW YORK · TORONTO · LONDON · SYDNEY · AUCKLAND

LOOKS LIKE LOVE

A Bantam Book / February 1994

*LOVESWEPT and the wave design are registered
trademarks of Bantam Books, a division of
Bantam Doubleday Dell Publishing Group, Inc.
Registered in U.S. Patent
and Trademark Office and elsewhere.*

*If you would be interested in receiving protective vinyl covers for your
Loveswept books, please write to this address for information:*

*Loveswept
Bantam Books
P.O. Box 985
Hicksville, NY 11802*

ISBN 0-553-44337-2

Published simultaneously in the United States and Canada

*Bantam Books are published by Bantam Books, a division of Bantam Dou-
bleday Dell Publishing Group, Inc. Its trademark, consisting of the words
"Bantam Books" and the portrayal of a rooster, is Registered in U.S. Patent
and Trademark Office and in other countries. Marca Registrada. Bantam
Books, 1540 Broadway, New York, New York 10036.*

PRINTED IN THE UNITED STATES OF AMERICA

OPM   0 9 8 7 6 5 4 3 2 1

This one's for
Candace Keegan Cowdrick
and Diane Pizzuta.
Looks like you've survived
another one!

ONE

Jill Stuart watched Max's eyes a moment more, then stole a glance toward the horizon. At most, she had another five minutes before the March sun rose on the island community off Florida's west coast. When had she lost control? She looked down at her scanty attire and immediately took a deep, calming breath. If she worked quickly and carefully, this fiasco would end before anyone in Cinnamon Key spotted her in her nightclothes.

Her thoughts were interrupted by an impatient growl. Pressing a hand to her collarbone, she took a step forward. The small white terrier continued chewing on her silk kimono and was now dragging it with him as he backed away.

Today was not the day for this. Not with little Andy coming. Not with the parrot funeral to plan. And certainly not with her boss, Mr. Merriweather, due for a "surprise" visit.

"Come on, Max. Let's go home. I'll give you a treat."

With his tail wagging like a metronome, Max flattened his forelegs to the ground. Lowering his chin to his paws, he shifted his eyebrows as he continued staring at her.

Studying his moves, Jill sensed the situation coming to a turning point, and the tension between her brows began to ease. She was going to regain control any moment now. Everything was going to be fine. It was simply a matter of reeling him in on the kimono. As she began reaching forward, she measured out her voice—half reasoning, half promising.

"That's right. We'll play a game. We'll—"

His tail slowed to a stop as he raised himself on all fours and stepped back. Jill eased herself down to a crouch and into a slow crawl over the dew-soaked grass. Any second now she'd have him. Any second.

As the sun began filtering through the screen of hibiscus, she winced at her miscalculations. Daylight was upon her, and she was still in her nightclothes pleading with ten pounds of mischief. Her control was slipping again. She closed her eyes to center her scattering thoughts.

"Please come home, Max. I'll give you anything you want. Anything."

The dog stopped backing up, cocked his head, and watched with growing curiosity.

So did the man in the window.

With a coffee mug in one hand and a portable phone in the other, Drew Webster pressed his nose against the glass. Who, he wondered, was this blond Venus kneeling in his uncle's backyard? And why was she begging Max to come home with her? He lowered the phone and twisted his head until his ear was flat against the glass. And why was she clad only in her lingerie?

"Drew? This is important," came the voice over the portable phone. "That casino in Atlantic City wants to talk about our proposal for their atrium. I told them we'd get back to them. Drew? Are you there?"

Atriums were the last thing on Drew's mind as he leaned his cheek against the window to get a better look at the mesmerizing tableau outside. She wasn't moving a muscle of her sleek and perfectly tanned body. The only thing in motion was the morning sunlight dancing through her white-blond hair. He smiled. So Venus had white-blond hair. Twisting his head again, he noticed that the pale pink of her tap pants and lace-edged chemise contrasted rather nicely with the shocking-red hibiscus. Shifting her hips, Venus began reaching out to something or someone beyond the window. His jaw dropped open at the same time one pink strap slipped from her shoulder. Drew set his mug down and pressed his forehead against the window for a better look, but the lady in pink was moving slowly out of sight.

"I'll get back to you, Jeff." Without taking his eyes from the scene outside, Drew clicked off the phone and tossed it onto the four-poster behind him. He straightened his tie and ran his fingers through his hair. The last thing he expected to find in his uncle's backyard was a love goddess.

"Max, I'm not playing anymore," he heard her wail as he opened the door.

She was hitting the grass with her hand. Shaking his head, he quietly crossed the patio to where she was sprawled on her stomach. He moved close enough to notice a trace of downy white hair between her shoulder blades and a tiny mole above the band of lace. With only a quick glimpse of her profile, he couldn't see much of her face. White-blond curls parted on the side and reaching just below her ears obscured it. Right now he'd have to be satisfied with the exquisite curves of her body and lean lines of her legs and arms. Lord, she was femininity from head to toes. And all that lovely sun-kissed skin interrupted by nothing more than sexy silk lingerie.

"Please don't run!" Jill lowered her head onto her forearm and hit the ground again. Things were definitely out of control. She should be in her office preparing for Mr. Merriweather's visit. And why had she promised to take little Andy miniature golfing?

Nearby she heard a door open, then shut. Several seconds later a pair of oxblood wing tips appeared in her peripheral vision.

"Never beg," instructed a masculine voice above her.

"What?"

"I said, never beg. Besides, he can't be worth it if he has you groveling in the dirt."

"I can't lose him. Shhh." Not bothering to look up at her uninvited adviser, she scrambled on all fours past the patio, then stopped. Sinking back on her heels, she shoved her fists to her hips. "Now you've done it. You've scared him away, and I'll never catch him."

She heard amusement mixed with uncertainty in the man's voice when he replied, "Catch him? Why would he ever want to run from you?"

Jill stood up and brushed the dew from her hands and legs. "It's just a game he likes to play," she said, straining her neck toward the picnic area. Whoever this man was, she wished he would quietly leave. He was breaking her concentration. She picked her kimono off the lawn, gave it a quick shake, and slipped it on. As she was about to turn to confront the stranger, a ball of white fur caught her eye.

"Some game he likes to play," the man remarked. Then, in a tone of disbelief, "A *dog*?"

Max had reappeared from behind a palm, launched himself inches into the air with an energetic bark, and tore off again.

With frantic energy Jill waved her hands in the air. "Not the canal, Max," she said in a fierce whisper as she sprinted after the dog.

Dashing through the backyards of Nutmeg Court, Jill recognized the signs of an awakening neighborhood. A few automatic sprinklers were on, and newspapers were already being retrieved from several lawns. One person waved at her. Pretty soon they'd all see her running through their backyards in dishabille and out of control. She began imagining the letters that would be written to Merriweather Development about this incident. She had to put the consequences out of her mind, though, because Max had just rounded the gazebo and would be at the canal any moment.

Jill stopped beside the large, bougainvillea-draped structure, trying once again to gather her thoughts and plan a new strategy.

"Is it always so lively around here in the morning?"

Hadn't *he* gone away yet? "Shhh. Of course not," she whispered.

"I thought Cinnamon Key would have a leash law."

Turning to him, she was about to explain that Cinnamon Key did have a leash law, because she'd written it. What she saw left her tongue attached to the roof of her mouth.

Her first impression was that he didn't belong there. Looking totally out of place in the 90-degree heat, he was still undeniably gorgeous in his three-piece business suit and Italian print tie. He looked as if he'd missed his jet to the polo matches but could call up another anytime he felt like it. That was an easy speculation considering he had the most confident, engaging smile she'd ever seen. Thick chocolate-brown hair swept back and to the side over his smoky topaz eyes. His gaze was magnetic, so magnetic, she couldn't stop staring. Who was this guy? Like a deer trapped in a headlight's beam, she found it impossible to look away. Finally, her gaze drifted down over the rest of his face. There was something roguish about the trace of dark stubble on his chin and jaw and the way it contrasted with the rest of his face.

Appearing to be in his early thirties, he was too young for a snowbird. So if he wasn't escaping the cold winter season up north, he had to be visiting one of the residents of Cinnamon Key. There was no other explanation. An alarm went off in her brain. No. It couldn't be one of Mr. Merriweather's associates. Suddenly conscious of her nightclothes, she pulled the kimono closer, retied the sash, and smoothed the lapels. He didn't *look* like the type usually accompanying Mr. Merriweather, but she had to ask anyway.

"You wouldn't be from Merriweather Development, would you?"

"Not unless you wanted me to be."

His outright flirting was disarming, but she forced herself to accept his answer as nothing more than a reprieve. Brushing away a lock of curly hair from her forehead, she sighed loudly. "I have to catch Max. What time is it?"

"Right. Max."

As he lifted his wrist to check the time, the man was barely concealing his amusement with the minidrama. Slipping both hands into his pockets, he leaned against the gazebo. "Almost six-thirty. Mind if I watch this?"

The twinkle in his eye was daring her and teasing her at the same time. When she moved the edge of her kimono to cover one knee, his gaze followed her hand, then continued slowly to her toes and back up her body. He'd meant for her to see the appreciation in his eyes. And in his slowly evolving smile. Her own nerve endings were humming with interest. Something delicious was stirring between them. Something rich and real in the perfumed morning air. The laugh lines around his eyes continued deepening. As she began returning his smile, Max barked, she blinked, and the moment was gone.

Was she losing her mind? She was standing in her nightclothes letting this stranger flirt with her when she should be off catching Max! "I'm sure you must find this all quite amusing. Well, it isn't going to stay funny for long if Max reaches the canal," she said, stomping away.

"Forgot his inner tube, did he?"

"Alligators," she shot back over her shoulder. The man suddenly stood to attention.

"Alligators? What alligators?"

"The Cinnamon Key Wildlife Sanctuary backs up to this community. The alligators are always swimming into our part of the canal and—Max!"

The little white dog rounded the gazebo and ran between them, punctuating every other step with a bark. He was like a windup toy wound too tightly. He also appeared to be having the time of his life.

Drew sized up the situation, which was close to chaotic. "To the right!" he shouted.

In a matter of seconds he headed off the dog, sending him straight to the lady in pink. Her look of relief as she scooped up Max was a visual delight. She was patting the happy creature, her pink nail polish and tanned fingers making an interesting contrast against the dog's back. With the tips of her fingers sunk into the white fur, it made Drew think of snow and Christmas. He began imagining her hand resting against his ski-sweatered chest. Then he pictured her hand drifting down—

Breaking into his thoughts, he heard her scold, "Bad dog, Max." Any corrective effect was lost when she allowed the dog to lick her chin. With relief still evident in her blue-green eyes, she looked up at him. "Thanks. I'm sorry, I didn't introduce myself. I'm Jill Stuart, the sales manager and resident liaison here at Cinnamon Key."

"Drew Webster. You're probably the person I want to see. I'm here visiting my uncle. Maybe you know him. Ralph Webster?"

Her thick blond brows lifted in amusement. "You're Ralph's nephew? You're little Andy?"

He pressed his hands together, then opened them and shrugged. "What can I say? I've been eating my Wheaties."

He certainly had. His broad shoulders didn't come from a padded suit, and that impish grin held a degree of sensuality that didn't quite fit the seven-year-old she was expecting.

"When he told me his nephew, Andy, was coming for a visit, I volunteered to help keep you busy. I'm supposed to take you golfing this afternoon. He didn't expect you until later."

He walked alongside her. His height, somewhere over six feet, was perfect for blocking her five-feet-eight-inch frame from Mr. Hernandez's line of vision.

Drew slid his hands into his pockets once again. After a sideways glance at her he decided not to touch her remark about keeping him busy. Sooner or later, though, he'd remind her of her promise to Uncle Ralph. "I was through with my business meetings in Atlanta earlier than I expected. Luckily, I was able to catch a ride on a friend's company jet at four this morning." Rubbing his chin, he began to add, "I didn't even take time to—"

She slapped a hand across his chest. "Don't move."

"I beg your pardon?" He looked at her hand and was instantly reminded of the image he'd had several minutes ago. Her pink-polished nails were a feminine counterpoint to the firm pressure she kept up against his shirt and tie.

"Oh, no." Wrapping her fingers around the knot in his tie, she led him behind a storage shed. "Sorry," she said, letting go of his tie. "Mr. Hernandez was about to see me." Covering her bottom lip with the edge of her teeth, she peeked around the corner of the building and held her breath. After a moment she slouched against the wall and exhaled. "Okay, he's gone. I'm sorry, what were you saying?"

Standing closer, Drew braced a hand on the wall next to her head. Max sniffed suspiciously. "Just that Uncle Ralph left his key and a note with the gatehouse guard. Seems he and a friend are in Miami. They're due back this afternoon. So-o-o . . ."

"So?" she asked as she watched his serious expression turn into a challenging grin.

"So what are we going to do to keep me busy?"

Her breath caught in her throat when all sorts of delicious images presented themselves to her. As if he were reading her mind, his eyebrows lifted in pretended shock. Ducking under his arm, she came out on the other side of him. When he looked over his shoulder, she was already backing away. "You're a big boy, Mr. Webster. And I have work to do. Thanks again for helping with Max."

"I'll walk you."

"No." She was hurrying now. "I mean, please don't go to that trouble."

"Wait. What about our golf date?"

"Tell Ralph I'm canceling that reservation at Rex World."

"Rex World?"

"He suggested I take little Andy miniature golfing."

"Then by all means don't disappoint little Andy," he called after her. "He loves miniature golfing."

She put a finger to her lips to quiet him. "I don't," she said, teasing him back. "I've really got to get Max home and then get ready for work."

"Jill?"

"Yes?"

He waited the longest time before answering. "What would you really like to do today?"

There it was again. That sensual challenge in his voice that belied the innocence of his words and stirred up the butterflies low in her belly. "To keep my job," she said, darting behind a house as its resident came out and hung up a bird cage on his carport. She waited for the man to go inside again before pulling on her robe. "I work here, Drew. This is getting embarrassing."

He nodded once as a businesslike tone returned to his voice. "Is your office in the building by the main gate?"

"Yes. Twenty-one Cinnamon Circle."

"I'd like to come up later and talk to you about something. Uncle Ralph's concerned about a problem he—"

"A problem? Is there something wrong with Ralph? He isn't ill, is he?"

"No. It's a security matter."

A security matter? That was all she needed on top of everything else. "What kind of security matter?"

"Hi, Jill. I like your new clothes."

Another resident had discovered her. Rolling her eyes, she lifted one of Max's paws, on her index finger, to wave it. "Max got out," she explained.

Returning her gaze to Drew, she felt her stomach contract. And not from hunger. Or the possibly worrisome situation he was about to explain. He was smiling at her. It wasn't a smug smile, or even the kind that enjoyed another's discomfort. It was the kind of smile that begged you to see the humor inherent in the moment and enjoy it with him. She bit her lip to keep from laughing out loud. He had her attention once again. All of her attention.

"You're a very popular lady around here," he said, strolling closer. "Tell me, should I take a ticket and wait my turn?"

His voice was deep and masculine, curling around her like a warm caress. Every fiber of her being locked into the intimacy of the moment. The humid air took on a misty quality, and only the light in his smoky topaz eyes shone through.

Something was happening to her, something warm and alive and—Max struggled in her tightening embrace. She blinked and looked down at the little dog. Rescued from the evolving fantasy, she felt the sting of a blush on her face. "What kind of security matter?" she repeated as Drew caught up with her.

"He thinks one of his neighbors is being systematically burglarized."

Jill amazed herself by keeping her lower jaw in the up position. He'd managed to melt her bones, then turn her stone-cold, both inside of one minute. Presenting a calm exterior to this man would be a minor miracle. She shook her head, fighting the crazy idea of crime in Cinnamon Key. "Someone would have reported a burglary to me. I'm sure there's been a mistake."

He shook his head firmly. "Not according to Uncle Ralph. Seems it's happened several times over the past three months."

She shook her head again. "This can't be true. Ralph has simply misinterpreted something." Of course it wasn't true, but a tiny shiver rippled through her body anyway. The mere thought of a burglary at Cinnamon Key was enough to make anyone shiver. Or was it that Drew Webster was moving closer?

"I know Uncle Ralph, and he's not the type to misinterpret this sort of thing. He's one of the most levelheaded people around." He ran his fingers through his thick, straight hair, combing it back from his forehead. "Look, I've come here because I'm very fond of him. I hate seeing him distressed, especially at his age. Jill, he's seventy-two years old, and I wouldn't want him to be next."

"Of course you wouldn't. Neither would I. But I find it seriously hard to believe there's a crime wave in progress here. My fingers are on the pulse of this community. These people are like family to me."

He reached out to give a gentle tug on Max's whiskers. The dog responded with a playful nip. With his thumb still in Max's mouth, Drew looked up.

"Then you can appreciate my concern for my uncle."

His steady gaze and serious expression shook her confidence. Maybe, just maybe, he was onto something that had escaped her attention. "Yes, I do appreciate your concern. Just who did Ralph say is the victim?"

"He didn't tell me."

When the backs of his fingers brushed her wrist, he left them there. The continuing contact was sending sparks flying through her, disorienting her. "How long will you be visiting Ralph?"

"I think I could stretch this visit into a week or more . . . with a little encouragement."

A week. A whole luscious week with Drew Webster down the street. What a provocative idea. She looked down at where his fingers were rubbing against her wrist.

"Jill, I'd hate to think of anyone in danger here. I want to help."

Danger?

Help?

His friendly attitude coupled with his determined sensuality had her breaking a sweat. Temptation never looked or felt so good. Then that old panic began spiraling in her stomach, and something akin to a warning flare went off inside her. The burgeoning sensations suddenly imploded to one nugget of truth. Right now Drew Webster was the danger. No matter that she felt herself drawn to him, she couldn't afford the luxury of seeing where the attraction could lead. She'd been disappointed by people before, and she wasn't about to take that risk again. Long ago she'd learned not to need anyone for anything; she'd learned to depend on herself. Wrapping her arms firmly around Max, she stepped away. She didn't know how she was going to do it, but she was going to check out his burglary story and avoid him at the same time. "There's really no need for you to stay the whole week. No one's in danger here, and if someone were, I'd take care of it. I take care of all the problems at Cinnamon Key. That's my job."

She turned away from him as he narrowed his eyes and scratched his chin. Heading for the side yard, she could feel him staring at her. Controlling her desire to run, she walked across the street to Barbara Brody's house. There were other things to occupy her mind besides Drew Webster. Like getting Max home.

Barbara met her at the door of her screened porch.

"Jill." The older woman pressed a fistful of pearl necklaces to her breast. "Where did you find Max?"

"I was out on my balcony having my morning coffee when I spotted him trotting toward the gatehouse."

"I had no idea he'd gotten out," Mrs. Brody said, looping the opera-length strings around the fingers of one hand. Taking Max from Jill, she hugged the tiny dog to her chin. "I know what a handful this little maniac can be once he gets going, and I can't thank you enough for bringing him back. I was up early this morning cleaning some jewelry and completely forgot about him."

While Barbara showered Max with embarrassing attention, Jill looked toward Ralph Webster's house. "It did take a little longer to catch him than I expected."

"Well, won't you come in for some coffee, dear? You probably didn't get a chance to finish yours." Max looked up from Mrs. Brody's arms and barked.

"Thanks for the offer, but I have to get back and dressed for work." She turned for the door, stopping before her hand reached the doorknob. "Mrs. Brody, how well do you know Ralph Webster?"

"Rather well. He's in my bridge club, and I've had him over several times for dinner. Why do you ask?"

The last thing she wanted to do was alarm the older woman. Recently widowed, Barbara Brody was trying valiantly to put her life back together. Unwarranted speculations about neighborhood crime would only cause the older woman needless worry. Still, Jill felt an obligation to the community to put Drew Webster's words to rest permanently. "I, uh, just met his nephew, and I was wondering if Ralph had ever said anything to you about him."

Barbara's exaggerated expression was meant to tease. "Andy? You met little Andy in your nightclothes?"

"He's no little Andy. He's probably in his early thirties and likes to be called Drew. What has Ralph said about him?"

"Not much. Only that he's from up North and Ralph doesn't see him often enough. They do talk on the phone at least once a week. Seems the boy's very involved in expanding his business." Barbara ran her fingertips over the little dog's nose. "For what this is worth, Jill, he's divorced. No children."

"Lots of people are divorced, Barbara," said Jill, a bit too quickly.

Tilting her head to one side, Barbara looked up at Jill. "So, what do you think of him?"

"He's . . . very interested in his uncle." Jill fixed her eyes on the pearls while she tried to figure out a way to slip in a question about the alleged burglaries. "He wants to make sure Ralph is safe here in Cinnamon Key. Isn't that funny? I mean, who doesn't feel safe in Cinnamon Key?"

While Barbara patted the back of her neatly chignoned hair, the strings of pearls dangled from her fingers, clicking softly. "I can't imagine."

"You've never seen anyone or anything suspicious around the neighborhood, have you?"

"Of course not, dear. Nothing of a suspicious nature happens here. But if it ever did,

I'd call you immediately, and you'd take care of it."

Breathing a sigh of relief, Jill nodded.

"You've always taken care of things so well, Jill."

Max barked, it seemed for emphasis, and the two women laughed.

"That's right, Max," Jill said, shaking her finger at the dog. "I take care of all the problems at Cinnamon Key. That's my job."

TWO

Drew tossed aside the shell collectors' magazine and stared across the office at her. Jill had been keeping him waiting for almost an hour, and if it weren't for the pleasing picture she made, he might have left long ago. He liked the way her tobacco-colored pumps made the curve of her calves more pronounced, and the way she held her cream-colored dress with the flat of her hands when she sat down. With her simple gold jewelry and long linen jacket, her appealing look was of tony smartness and controlled confidence.

Remembering her different look that morning, Drew sensed the stirrings of a physical response and shifted in his seat. Ah, there! He'd caught her eye again. He winked and thought he saw a hint of pink stain her cheeks a second later. She was looking back at the couple sitting beside her desk. Tilting her head, she was trying to appear totally absorbed in what the man was saying. Her ploy almost worked, but another glance toward Drew betrayed her. He congratulated himself; his presence was unnerving her. Reconfirming his decision to stay put, he settled back in the chair. She was worth the wait.

Meanwhile, the bored woman in the too-tight jumpsuit checked the fit of her acrylic nails, then admired them as her husband droned on.

"Jill, baby, the wife and me don't like palm trees. The place we could be interested in has six of 'em, and too many ratty palmettos out back too." He placed his hands firmly on the desk. "Cut down the palms, get rid of the bushes, and we'd maybe consider buying here."

"Mr. Randall, two defining elements of our community are the palm trees and the lush tropical vegetation. Our residents lease their lots from Merriweather Development, and those two items are not negotiable. Perhaps I could suggest that you consider the community of Aruba Sunrise. It's over on the mainland and, from what I've seen of it, has absolutely no plant life." Jill gestured to a paper between them. "I'd be happy to point it out to you on this map."

Drew shook his head as he watched and listened. How in the world she managed to maintain her composure was beyond him. Her stonewalling was admirable, especially since she'd accomplished it with a silky voice and charming manner. He added unrelenting confidence to that list when she stood up to show them out.

Jill closed the door on the obnoxious couple. As difficult as they'd been to get rid of, she was even more concerned that it was Drew Webster who hadn't given up and left her office. Being ignored for almost an hour apparently hadn't fazed him. How tenacious, she wondered, was he going to be about those "burglaries"? Too bad for him that he didn't know he was wasting his time. If there were any problems to be checked on in Cinnamon Key, she was going to be the one doing the checking. Not Drew Webster. She took a deep breath, then turned around to face him.

He stood up, and as he walked toward her, she was once again reminded of how tall he was. And good-looking. His tan shorts and forest-green three-button shirt had a pricey, casual look to them. And she'd seen the expensive brand of his leather boating shoes before. By the well-worn look of his, he must have loved them for their comfort and not their ability to impress.

"Sorry to keep you waiting. Drew, wasn't it?"

He gave her a slightly disappointed frown. "My playmates call me Andy."

Fighting a smile, she returned to the safety of her desk. Allowing herself the enjoyment of his humor was an extravagance she shouldn't be permitting herself. She had a career to preserve, not to mention a way of life she was sufficiently satisfied with. She didn't need Drew Webster invading it. Lifting the edge of her sleeve, she looked at her watch. "Has your uncle Ralph returned yet?"

When Drew didn't answer, she looked up. He'd been waiting for her full attention, and now that he had it, he was thoroughly enjoying it.

"No. As a matter of fact, he called a while ago. He and his friend were having car trouble. They'll be getting in late tonight."

She nodded slowly. Ralph Webster was one of the most capable men she knew. Still, she was always uneasy when one of her residents was in any kind of trouble. And she wanted to talk to Ralph soon about this burglary business. "I'm sure they'll be fine."

Drew walked toward her as she riffled through a stack of pamphlets on her desk. He must have heard that touch of skepticism she thought she'd managed to keep out of her voice.

"Uncle Ralph's ridden camels across North Africa and a Jeep over the Andes. I suspect engine trouble in Miami won't do him in."

He was about to say more, but she cut in. "There's no need to waste the day, Drew. I have maps of the area and pamphlets on some of South

Florida's most popular tourist attractions." She held them out.

He took them, thumbed through them in an undisguised gesture of courtesy, and placed them back on the desk.

"No, thanks."

Fiddling busily with the sleeves of her suit jacket, she found her thoughts turning to Peter. He would love seeing this determined man giving his sister a hard time. Picking up a paper from the desk, she found herself imagining what Peter would say about Drew. "Hangs on good, Sis. How can you fault a guy for that?" Then he would chuck her on the chin and laugh that easy laugh. Every time she thought about Peter studying to be a doctor, her heart filled with pride. Her gaze drifted up to Drew, and she found herself gritting her teeth. How much longer would Drew "hang on"? she wondered. After a moment he leaned across the desk, took the paper from her, and turned it right side up. As he placed it in her hands again, he sat down.

The radio was playing a soft samba. He lifted one foot onto his knee and tapped out the rhythm on his ankle. With an inward sigh she wondered how she was going to maintain a shield of aloofness when he insisted on treating it as nothing more than a comical veneer. She was supposed to be ignoring him in order to get rid of him, but that was impossible since everything about him was so disarmingly straightforward. Even that wink. He was hard not to like and impossible to ignore. Jill placed the paper on the desk. She'd have to try harder. "Look, I've got a ton of things to do and—"

"I'm making you nervous, aren't I?"

No smoke screen here, she thought. His arrow had hit the mark. Her palms were sweating as she pushed for a shrug and sat down. "Nervous? Of course you're not making me nervous."

He pointed over his shoulder with his thumb. "Maybe it was the happy home-buyers, then. You took care of them like a pro. I would have stopped being civil long before he started haggling over the palm trees."

It was an undisguised compliment, and she decided to accept it. Not many people had witnessed this side of her job, and the few who had probably didn't understand the delicate maneuvering it required. Folding her hands on the edge of the desk, she hoped she was looking appropriately humble. "I deal with all sorts of people in this job. Sooner or later they would have left. Anyway, I don't think they'll be back."

"Was that your objective with me when you kept me waiting for nearly an hour?" He lifted his eyebrows and held them in a mocking pose as he continued tapping out the samba rhythm on his ankle.

A smile froze on her face. He'd tricked her. With that savvy mind and sexy grin, he'd tricked her. Well, he wasn't going to get away with it. She took hold of the edge of her desk and forced a laugh that sounded artificial even to her. "That's ridiculous. I haven't been trying to get rid of you."

"Glad to hear it." He dropped his foot to the floor and leaned forward. "Now let's discuss that phone call Uncle Ralph made to me about these burglaries."

She shook her head, making her smart cut move in a very unbusinesslike way. Stiffening her spine, she patted down the side of her hair. "I think there's been some mistake. This neighbor of Ralph's probably lent out a few things to a friend, forgot about them, then mentioned something to your uncle about not being able to place his or her hands on the things." She nodded, hoping Drew wouldn't interpret it as condescension. "And maybe Ralph exaggerated this to you in order to get his favorite nephew down here for a visit. Wouldn't you say that's a strong possibility, Drew?" She didn't wait for him to answer. Stacking several folders, she carried them to the file cabinet behind the desk. That ought to quiet his suspicions, she thought, as she slipped the folders into the drawer.

His hand closed over her wrist as she was about to shut the drawer.

"No, I would not say that's a strong possibility. My uncle is not a lonely old man who must resort to lying in order to see me. If he says there's a problem here, then I believe him. You said this morning that you take care of everything. Why aren't you taking care of this?"

"Because no one has said anything to me about any burglaries."

"Well, I am now. First, I'd like to know about security around here."

Those eyes of his were the last thing she wanted to look into. Instead, she fixed her gaze on his hand and the dark, springy hair on the back of it. If he were holding her wrist too tightly, she could jerk it away, but unfortunately that wasn't the case. The pad of his thumb pressed softly against her pulse point, while the rest of his hand covered hers, warming it. She hadn't expected the calluses, and if the moment were friendlier, she would have asked how he'd gotten them. But it wasn't a friendly moment. Just an incredibly intimate one. She closed her eyes.

"Our security is quite adequate."

After a moment he released her wrist, and she slid the drawer shut as if nothing important had passed between them. But something had happened in those few moments, and with the warmth of his touch still lingering, she found it difficult to focus her thoughts. Her own voice surprised her as she spoke: shaky and soft, yet somehow defiant. "You ought to be out enjoying this lovely weather instead of—"

He offered his hand, and she accepted. It would have been just a courteous gesture, a finalizing move to an uncomfortable situation, except for one thing. For the first time since she'd met him, his face was without humor. In fact, his expression was cool and formal. "Thanks for your time, Miss Stuart. I won't be taking up any more of it."

He turned to go, and a feeling of unease tingled through her. "Wait. What are you going to do?"

"What else can I do? I'm going to find out what's going on. When I do, I'll call in the police."

"The police?" Like a fickle friend, control began slipping from her camp to Drew's. She hurried around to the other side of the desk, praying he couldn't sense the panic she felt exploding through her skin. She willed herself to speak in a normal conversational tone. "Shouldn't you at least talk to your uncle before you think about bringing the police into it? I know I'd like to talk to Ralph."

"I plan to. Meanwhile, I'm going to do some investigating on my own. I'm sure I'll be able to find people willing to talk to me," he said, starting for the door once again.

"Drew, I wish you wouldn't do that. I don't want anyone alarmed unnecessarily."

"That's not my purpose, Jill."

"But I'm afraid that's what will happen." She moved away from the desk and toward a table model of Cinnamon Key. Complete with miniature houses, meandering streets and canals, and tiny palm trees, it looked perfectly secure and peaceful. Drew joined her by the model. "You see, our community is comprised of people fifty and older. Most are retired, and many donate a portion of their time to charities or volunteer at the local schools and hospitals. They've all worked hard to get to a point in their lives where they can have peace of mind and still lead productive lives. You can't blow in here like a blizzard, disrupting everything, when you don't know the whole story. We really don't know if there have been any crimes committed. Drew, I'm very skeptical about all this because none of the residents has said anything to me."

He pursed his lips for a long moment and appeared to be reconsidering his plans.

She hurried on. "Look, you don't know me, and you don't owe me anything, but you're going to make my job here a lot harder if you start stirring up unwarranted suspicions. These people are not prone to panic, but I think you should have all your facts together before you say anything. Before this gets out of hand, won't you let me talk to your uncle? Won't you at least give this another day?"

He nodded. "Okay. I'm spending the rest of the week here. One day won't matter."

His smile was back, shaking her to her toes. It was a generous smile that accepted truces and compromises, and she was surprised by how much she'd missed it in these last few minutes. "Thank you."

"My pleasure."

She was breathing through her mouth, and her palms were moist again. When he looked back at the table model of Cinnamon Key, the disorienting tension continued. She couldn't take her eyes away from him, and he couldn't take his eyes off the table model. There had to be a way to get his mind off this burglary thing, something that he wouldn't mistake for a flirtation. Rolling her pencil between her palms, she coughed softly. "So what kind of work do you do?"

"Why don't we have dinner tonight? I'll tell you then." His gaze swept across the table model and up to her face.

He was back to being his straightforward self. Those long-lashed eyes were radiating their charm and beginning to dazzle her resolve. If she wasn't careful, she'd be accepting a date with him. The thought set her heart to an erratic beat. Her life was at last predictable and secure, and somehow she knew if Drew Webster got into it, anything could happen. She looked down at the tips of her shoes. "I can't. I have a previous commitment."

He stepped closer. Close enough so that his daring reply was a whispered command. "Break it."

She laughed softly but kept her gaze glued to her shoes. "I can't get out of it."

"Sure you can."

"I promised I'd go."

"Then take me too."

Each of his comebacks was like a tiny, well-aimed tickle. He was the most outrageous flirt she'd ever met. She leaned her head toward her shoulder and considered the preposterous idea. If anyone could handle tonight's agenda, Drew Webster was probably the one. And if she took him along, she'd be able to keep an eye on him. "Under one condition."

"What's that?"

"That you won't bring up this burglary thing tonight."

"Agreed."

"Then meet me at my place at five o'clock." She pointed to the ceiling. "I live over the shop. Use the staircase around back by the parking lot. And don't bother to change clothes. What you're wearing is perfect."

Right at five Drew turned onto the crushed-shell path beside the only two-story building in Cinnamon Key, 21 Cinnamon Circle. The efficient, in-charge Jill Stuart seemed like the last person to encourage a three-party date for herself. She had surprised him. Then again, he chuckled to himself, she had been wearing lingerie when they'd met, and what could be more surprising than that? The crunching sounds beneath his feet continued as he rounded the corner into the parking lot. There, he found several people standing around talking with their bicycles in hand. Some waved, and as he headed up the stairs, he waved back at them.

Jill was out on the landing and closing her door before he was halfway up.

"You're right on time."

She looked terrific trotting down the stairs in her tropical-print shorts and tangerine camp shirt. Her white-framed sunglasses were perched on her head, and she held a gardening tool in one hand and a shoe box under her arm.

As she reached him, he detected a faint trace of raspberries and roses.

"Follow me."

Inhaling her fragrance again, he whispered, "Anywhere."

As she tied the shoe box to the back of her bicycle with a bungee cord, she began a series of introductions.

"You'll meet Mr. Henley a little later," she concluded as she slipped the trowel underneath the stretchy rope.

"A luau? Is that what we're doing for dinner?" he asked good-naturedly. "We'll be digging a pit?"

"'Fraid not." She pointed to a bicycle propped against the building. "That one's for you."

He nodded and, looking around, spotted more boxes secured to the other bicycles. "A boxed supper then?"

"No."

"Do I do the whole twenty questions, or are you going to tell me where we're going?"

She checked the watch on her wrist. "A funeral."

"A funeral? Dressed like this?"

She shrugged, and several people laughed. "We're all wearing dark glasses. So are you."

"This is a joke. Right?"

"Wrong. Unfortunately, Mr. Henley's parrot, Susie, died yesterday. She was a real character. He used to bring her to all our social functions at the clubhouse."

He held up his hand. "Don't tell me. She could swear a blue streak."

"Oh, no. Susie never talked. But she could sing the themes from *The Brady Bunch* and *The Addams Family.*"

One woman adjusted her visor. "And she was learning to hum the *Jeopardy* theme."

"Right, Jesse." She turned back to Drew as she got on her bicycle. "We're going to have a little service, spread some birdseed, and then we're all going to dinner. Ready?"

Five minutes later Jill and the group stopped their bicycles a few hundred yards inside the Cinnamon Key Wildlife Sanctuary.

"I didn't know you could bury pets inside these sanctuaries," Drew commented as he helped her remove the gardening tool and box from the back of her bicycle.

"You can't. This is illegal. Careful with the box."

Before Drew could say anything, she turned to the man walking toward them. "Hello, Mr. Henley. Have you been here long?"

His eyes were red-rimmed, but his voice was steady. "A bit. How did everything go?"

She stepped away from Drew, leaving him holding the box. From the weight of it he imagined a couple of pounds of birdseed. A thoughtful gesture on Jill's part, and it didn't surprise him. She appeared to have a sincere affection for these people.

"Fine. Everything's been taken care of, just like you wanted."

The elderly man nodded in thanks. "She was quite a party animal, wasn't she, Jill?"

Jill reached out and squeezed his arm. Her remarks were to Mr. Henley, but she looked toward the others as she spoke. "I'll never forget the first time I met her. It was at the Fourth of July picnic at the gazebo. My first week on the job, almost three years ago. Susie had just sung the theme from *The Addams Family*, and then she leaned over and bit me."

Several people laughed along with Mr. Henley.

"Mr. Henley, this is Drew Webster, Ralph's nephew. Ralph's still in Miami. I thought Susie's funeral would be cheerier for Drew than sitting around waiting for him. You don't mind, do you?"

Cheerier? Had she actually said "cheerier"? He'd heard of bizarre funeral rituals, but they usually involved small children, bathrooms, and goldfish. Surely, Jill had, as the politicians were prone to say, misspoken herself. Drew tucked the box under his arm and shook Mr. Henley's hand.

"Sorry about your bird." Lord, how inane he sounded.

He looked around him, expecting, for some undetermined reason, to see somber faces. The group mingled in a small clearing bordered by mangroves and sea grape; somberness appeared to be the last thing on their minds. The next few minutes were some of the strangest of Drew's thirty-three years. While small Styrofoam coolers were being opened, Mr. Henley considered a spot.

Wiping his eyes, the old man finally pointed to a soft sandy hill. "I think right about here, Jill?"

Mr. Henley walked to one of the coolers, and Drew waited for the old gent to lift out the bird. When Drew looked at Jill, a wave of compassion swept over him. By the warm and steady look she was returning, it was obvious she approved of his respectful attitude. She motioned for Drew to come closer, but when he placed the shoe box he'd been holding on the ground, her eyes narrowed in disapproval. Now what had he done? he wondered.

"Don't leave her there, Drew."

"Her?" Drew looked at Mr. Henley. He'd just taken a wine cooler from the Styrofoam container and was twisting off the top. Drew looked down at the box at his feet. He'd been carrying the corpse. Swallowing slowly, he brought the box and tool to Jill as he leveled an "I'll get you for this" look at her.

While the funeral guests toasted the bird's contumacious personality, Jill scraped the earth with the trowel. After several minutes of digging, the hole was still too shallow. Drew reached for the trowel.

"I can do it," she said, but relinquished the tool to his outstretched hand. As he worked, Jill provided him a running commentary on the situation. "Mr. Henley would have dug this himself, but his arthritis has been giving him fits lately. He's a widower. He volunteers his time at our library cataloguing donated books. Susie was good company for him. He's taking this pretty well."

Drew sized up the box, then continued digging. "Why is he burying Susie here?"

"He once told me he wondered if Susie ever thought about being in the wild. When he called to tell me she'd died, he said he wanted her buried here as a symbolic gesture. He also said he wanted to celebrate her life and spirit, not dwell on the fact that she was gone. That's why we're drinking wine coolers. I went by last night and picked up Susie and her cage cover. I sewed a little bag from it and—"

He was feeling somewhere between stunned and amazed, and he knew his face was sending that message clearly to Jill. Did these people have any idea how fortunate they were to have this woman's love and loyalty? He'd given up hope of having anything like that a long time ago. Before he said anything, she quickly went on.

"If you don't understand how important this is to him, I won't hold it against you. Just please don't laugh."

"Oh ye of little faith," Drew muttered under his breath.

Later, at the Flamingo Cafe, the partying began in earnest. Spirited reminiscences about the parrot were mixed with community chatter, the price of gasoline, a need for a third tennis court, and Mr. Henley's search for more hardcover books for the library. The boisterous group drew several stares from other patrons inside the pink-on-pink cafe. Feeling welcomed and surprisingly content, Drew began discussing alternative landscaping after one man complained about the amount of water needed to maintain his lawn.

He leaned back in the large curved booth and looked across the table. Jill was ga-gaing over someone's photo of a grandchild. It was apparent she was saying all the right things because the grandmother was agreeing emphatically with her. Raising her head to laugh, Jill's sparkling look connected with his. What passed between them happened in a second. A warm look of sharing, a feeling of rightness, a certain knowledge that all was well. Yes, he wanted to say, I am having a helluva fun time, and thank you for bringing me. She turned and the moment slipped away into an onslaught of good-natured teasing by those who'd seen it.

Back at her apartment door, she placed the trowel on the landing and waved good-bye to the rest of the party. Looking down the street after the receding group, she spoke to Drew. "You were a good sport about tonight. I don't know how to thank you."

He stepped closer. "Ask me in for coffee, and I'll help you think of something."

Opening the door, she waved for him to follow.

"I can't believe this," he said as he followed her in and watched her turn on a lamp.

Stroking the clear glass base, she smiled proudly. "It is a pretty lamp, isn't it? I picked the shells up here and a few over on Sanibel. It was fun arranging them."

"Jill, I mean I can't believe you didn't lock your door tonight. Anyone could have gotten in here. And where's that little dog of yours? Shouldn't he be tearing off my ankle by now?"

"You mean Max?"

"Yes."

"Oh, he's not my dog. He'd run off from a neighbor's this morning, and I was just catching him before he got into real trouble. Decaf or regular?"

Drew clasped his hands behind him and decided to back off for the time being. He couldn't change the fact that she'd left the door unlocked. He could only change the mood of the moment, which was light at least, and promising at most. There would be time to talk about this later.

"Decaf."

"Make yourself at home. I'll have it ready in a moment."

As good a time as he'd had, he was even happier that he finally had her alone again. In a purely masculine moment of triumph he eased himself onto a textured white cushion on one of the sofas, sighed loudly, and looked around. With arched doorways and two white columns separating the dining room from the living room, there was an open, airy Mediterranean look to the place. Several good pieces of bleached-pine furniture surrounded a seafoam-green area rug. The square table in front of the sofa held a personal-accounts journal, a paperback novel with two lovers in an inspiring clinch, and a basket filled with toy soldiers. Picking up a handful for closer inspection, he saw they were Civil War soldiers, both North and South. He spent the next few minutes lining them up for battle.

"Did you leave?" she shouted from the kitchen.

"No. I was just reviewing my strategy for our next encounter."

"Pardon me?"

"I said, you have a great place here." As he looked toward the kitchen, a framed photograph of Jill with her arms around a teenager caught his attention. He was about to ask who the handsome boy was when he saw Jill standing in the doorway clutching a can of coffee. He thought he saw the tiniest sign of tension appear, then disappear, from around her eyes.

"We never got to talk about your work, Drew. Why don't you come in here and have a seat."

"Had you sat closer to me during dinner, you would have learned that I'm a landscape architect in New Jersey," he began as he followed her into the kitchen. "Webster's Landscaping and Gardening Services, the definitive word in outdoor design. I design atriums, courtyards, corporate greens, things like that."

He straddled a chair, leaned his chin on the high back, and undertook the leisurely task of drinking in every detail of her. She'd kicked off her shoes and was padding around the kitchen. He noticed that the toenails of her slender feet were painted a pearly pink and that her earrings were tiny diamond studs that winked when she moved. She'd dropped her sunglasses on the table, and he picked them up. They were still warm from resting on her head. He slipped them on and continued watching her. In a dark room or lighted room, she had a marvelous glow about her.

"How's the landscaping business up there in New Jersey?" she asked as she poured boiling water through the coffeemaker.

He was imagining a darker room with the two of them in it when she asked the question. Sliding the glasses to the end of his nose, he raised his chin and narrowed his eyes. "I'm sorry. What were you saying about business?"

"We're all crazy about our gardens and yards down here," she said, handing him a fruit cookie. "Do people up there take a big interest in theirs?"

"Absolutely." He took off her glasses and set them on the table. "People don't seem to travel as much as they used to, and because of that, their personal surroundings have become all the more valuable to them. Private gardens are my personal favorite, but the bulk of our business is still commercial landscaping."

"'Our' business? Then you don't work alone?"

"I have twenty-four employees. Three of us are accredited by the American Society of Landscape Architects. Last year I opened three other offices. One in Delaware and two in Pennsylvania. Business has been so good, I've been scouting other states for an additional office." He popped the cookie into his mouth and chewed it thoughtfully. "Truth is, I've been letting business rule my life too much over the last few years. Uncle Ralph's been retired from the State Department and back in the States for some time, and I hardly ever see him. He's about the only family I have left, and I've been damn selfish with my time. I'm almost glad this burglary business came up, so I can spend some time with him."

Jill eyed him pointedly. "Sugar? Milk?"

"Black's fine."

Handing him both mugs, she picked up the bag of cookies, then crooked her finger for him to follow.

"Let's take these out on the balcony. There's a beautiful view of the Gulf from there, and this time of night, there's usually a breeze."

She turned off most of the lights inside; then, sliding open the screen door, she gestured for him to pass. After maneuvering through her balcony furniture, he bumped his head on a string of Japanese lanterns. They were half-hidden under the scalloped edge of the canvas awning.

"Quite, um, colorful," he commented, cocking his chin at the lanterns. They were cheap and gaudy, and no self-respecting interior designer would have allowed them anywhere near this place. There could be only one or two explanations for them. Maybe a children's party, though her having one at night on a balcony in a retirement community was doubtful. Instead, he pictured the plastic lanterns lighting a spirited gathering of close friends who shared a sense of the outrageous.

"Those were leftover from a party I had . . . a long time ago."

"Party?" he asked, setting down her coffee.

She didn't answer him right away. Instead, she set the bag of cookies down and leaned her elbows on the railing. Colored squares of lantern light were reflecting on the wide balustrade beside her elbows. Breezes coming off the water sent the scalloped edge flapping above them. Across the street the palms rustled restlessly.

As he drank his coffee, he watched her taking in the scene before them. She inhaled the coffee aroma, then tested the drink with the tip of her tongue before she sipped it. Without a doubt she was the most exquisite creature he'd ever seen. He was a rich man; he alone would own this moment forever.

He had little time to savor the thought, because as he continued watching her, her expression changed. She'd altered her focus and was obviously concentrating on a memory. Whatever that memory was, it had taken her out of the present. Drew's mouth went dry, and his heart pounded. He wanted her there with him.

"I don't know why I rehung the lanterns. That party was a long time ago and someplace else."

"It's good to have souvenirs from a happy time." His gaze met hers, and the moment floated around them, right and comfortable. After a few seconds she turned back to the Gulf.

"It's such a lovely view, isn't it?"

"The loveliest," he said as he continued staring at her. He was near enough to detect the scent of roses and raspberries. Near enough to touch her. Near enough to know he wanted her nearer. Much nearer.

She gave him a scolding look that was meant to lighten the mood. "I was talking about that," she said, pointing toward the moonlit water and dark palms.

He turned his back on the Gulf and rested his elbows on the rail. "I wasn't." Before she could reply, he went on. "You have a satisfying life here in Cinnamon Key, don't you?"

"I do." She nodded. "I really do, Drew. We have a sense of community here. A lot of caring. A lot of sharing."

He dropped his head back and watched the rippling edge of the awning.

"From what I've seen so far, it looks as if your life is all about caring for others. About seeing to their needs. Helping Mr. Henley with the bird. Chasing after Max this morning. Keeping obnoxious people out of here. What a sense of satisfaction you must have when you come home each evening." He set down his coffee and turned to her. Her fingers were still clinging to the railing, but she'd straightened out her arms. She licked her lips as he edged closer. "Is that how it is, Jill?"

"Yes, I'm very satisfied with my life."

He reached out and, with the tips of his fingers, turned her face in his direction. "There's just one thing I don't understand," he said, her platinum strands teasing at his hand.

"What's that?" She nervously licked her lips again.

"All this caring, all this involvement." He moved closer. "All this giving. Who takes care of you, Jill? Who sees to your needs?"

Her lips parted, but she didn't answer. It didn't matter to him if she even had an answer, because right now he didn't care to hear it. Leaning down, he brushed feather-light kisses across her lips. Touching her was intoxicating, and his sensible intentions began drowning in a sea of sensations. Roses and raspberries and her sweet mouth. His head dipped down again, and in a series of teasing caresses, he beckoned her at the borders of affection and lust. Drawing her closer, he continued shamelessly.

Their foreheads touched. "Who kisses you like this, Jill?" He lifted her chin, and she closed her eyes. Had she been thinking about another man? Was she wanting him now? He wanted to know. As he kissed her again, her arms went around him, and her lips parted to take him in. He'd anticipated the silken moisture inside, but not what it would do to him. She was sending him up in flames with each throaty sound she made. When she moved against him, impacting softly on every inch of him, he forced himself up for air. Just enough to ask again, "Who?"

When she opened her eyes, she was looking directly into his. Her gaze slid away to his shoulder. "No one," she whispered.

It should have been total triumph for his male ego to hear that reply, but it wasn't. Those two words held a multitude of meaning. Desire. Confession. Loneliness. Sweet longing. And now he felt like a bastard for asking.

He eased her out of his arms and ran a hand through his hair. "Maybe I was—"

The awkward moment shattered when a sharp beep sounded from below the balcony. A familiar voice called out, "Andy, is that you up there with Jill?"

He laughed aloud at the absurdity of being discovered, like two young teenagers, by his uncle. "Yes, Uncle Ralph. I'll be home soon."

Jill leaned over the rail and waved. "How was your trip, Ralph? That's a rental car, isn't it?"

He nodded. "Exhausting, Jill. Murphy's Law all the way. What could go wrong, did."

Jill turned to Drew. "I'll talk to your uncle tomorrow about this burglary business. He sounds as if he needs some sleep."

Drew took her hands in his. "Walk me to your door?"

She nodded, leading him off the balcony and into her apartment. "I'm glad they're back safely."

The scent of coffee lingered in the apartment. As they walked through, he noticed his impression on the sofa cushion, her shoes lying haphazardly by the kitchen door, and the toy soldiers, armed and at the ready. The only thing out of sync with the relaxed scene was Jill. He'd unnerved her out there on the balcony, and he sensed she was still shaken. When they got to the door, she stepped away and leaned against the wall.

"I hope everything went well for them in Miami, Drew. I know you'll think it's strange, but I feel better when they return to Cinnamon Key."

"Uncle Ralph and his friend?"

"Any of the residents. I feel better when they're here. Safer."

Nodding, he studied her for a long, quiet moment before he spoke. "I'll tell Uncle Ralph you want to talk to him. Promise me you'll lock this door when I leave."

She cocked her head. "But I never do, and I don't see why I should start now."

Opening the door, he set the lock. "Because someone is robbing the neighborhood."

"That has yet to be proven. You'll have to give me a better reason."

Looking up in frustration at the ceiling, he laughed silently. "Then how about this?" He went to her again, pressing one more kiss to her lips. She was making that little sound in her throat when he finally lifted his head. "Because with me around, you'd better lock your door."

He was all hard where she was soft, all giving where she was wanting, and already gone by the time she opened her eyes. With her lips still tingling from his kiss, she pushed away from the wall and headed for the balcony with a sigh of exasperation. Drew was leaving within the week, and then she wouldn't have to be concerned with this purely physical attraction-reaction anymore. Okay, maybe with his straightforward charm and savvy wit, he'd caught her interest in more than just a physical way.

Stepping out onto the balcony, she went to the rail and picked up his coffee mug. Whom was she kidding? It was the memory of his whispered questions bringing back those poignant feelings in her heart.

Who takes care of you? Who kisses you like this?

Leaning her elbow on the rail, she watched him walk in and out of lamplight toward his uncle's house. "No one," she whispered. "Not now. Not ever."

Of the few relationships she'd had, the sum of them all hadn't stirred her the way Drew's kisses did. Pressing his coffee mug to her lips, she smiled in spite of her pragmatic nature. There had been times when she'd thought about a Prince Charming coming to her rescue. A gorgeous guy with a sense of humor, a sensitive soul, and the ability to make *her* feel cared for. That hadn't happened while she'd been raising her younger brother, Peter, and putting herself through college. Her aura of responsibility and self-sufficiency had kept the fun-loving types away, while conversely drawing those wanting the same kind of attention she gave her brother, Peter. What had looked like several opportunities at good relationships had ended up dismal disappointments.

She pulled Drew's coffee mug away from her lips. Peter was in medical school, she reminded herself as she set the mug on the rail. She had a great job that was keeping him there and providing an adequate enough life for her. This burglary thing was a minor bump in the road. She would take care of it; she didn't need or want anyone interfering. Certainly not anyone who made her doubt how satisfied she was with her life. Certainly not Drew Webster.

"My playmates call me Andy," he'd said.

Straining for a last glimpse of him, she chewed the edge of her thumbnail and remembered his antics. He was quick to laugh at himself. That moment at dinner after they'd caught each other's eye and several people had teased him, he'd made a face and shrugged his shoulders. She laughed out loud as she recalled it but quickly covered her mouth with her fingers. These continuing reactions to Drew were ridiculous. He'd be gone within the week, and her life would continue on course at Cinnamon Key. Mood swings weren't her style, anyway, she told herself, as she picked up both mugs and the bag of cookies and headed for the kitchen.

THREE

Checking her watch for the third time, Jill continued pacing in front of the strip mall. Now that she'd had time to think about Drew's burglary story, she couldn't *stop* thinking about it. Could it be possible that Ralph knew of something as sinister as burglaries taking place over a three-month period, and she hadn't gotten wind of them yet? At the very least, she couldn't pretend it wasn't possible. Shaking her wrist, she checked her watch again. Anything was possible, but one thing was certain—saving Merriweather Development a few dollars on computer paper by driving five miles inland to Macomber was proving to be false economy. She looked again at the Closed sign on Ink Spot Discount Office Supplies and silently cursed the time she was wasting. She'd give Ink Spot another ten minutes to open, and then it was back to Cinnamon Key and straight to Drew's uncle with a ton of questions.

Wiping a film of perspiration from her brow, she glanced over at the sign in the window of Dilby's Pawnshop. FULLY AIR CONDITIONED. By the look of the rusty unit protruding from the front window, she doubted it was efficient enough to stop the perspiration trickling down her spine. Still, a walk through the pawnshop might take her mind off things.

Wincing at the electric bell announcing her entrance, she stepped quickly into the pawnshop and shut the door.

"'Morning. I'll be with you in a minute," the man behind the counter said.

She waved to acknowledge his greeting, but the man had already chomped on his cigar, redirected his attention to his calculator, and resumed his conversation with his customer. As Jill looked at the guitar display hanging from the ceiling, she couldn't help overhearing their conversation.

"Sorry, ma'am, but I can't go that high."

"Surely, you can reconsider, Mr. Dilby. We've been doing business for months now. Just look at these pearls. They're opera length and perfectly matched, as you can see. My husband bought them in Majorca." Barbara Brody's voice quivered for control. "I wouldn't be here if I didn't need the money."

Barbara Brody? Jill whirled around. "Barbara? What are you doing here?" she whispered. But Barbara Brody had already answered that question. "*I wouldn't be here if I didn't need the money.*"

Gasping, the older woman turned to face her, then grabbed for the sunglasses hanging on a cord around her neck and hurriedly shoved them on. "Oh, no . . ."

Barbara Brody dropped her chin as she turned back to Mr. Dilby. For a long, uncomfortable moment no one spoke. Mr. Dilby broke the silence. "Okay, Mrs. Brody, I can let you have eight hundred."

Jill felt the older woman's embarrassment. Part of her wanted to leave quickly and save Barbara Brody any more of it. Then Barbara's shoulders dropped, and she spoke in a defeated, papery-thin voice.

"Thank you. That will be fine, Mr. Dilby."

As Mr. Dilby wrote up the ticket and counted out the cash, Barbara slipped the pearls into their velvet sack and pushed it across the counter. "I'll be back for them," she said, taking the ticket and the money and shoving both into her shoulder bag.

"Barbara?" Stepping forward, Jill touched her on the elbow. She continued softly. "Barbara, do you want to join me next door for a cup of coffee?"

At first Barbara shook her head; then she seemed to change her mind and nodded lethargically. "Yes."

Several minutes later Barbara Brody took off her sunglasses, folded them, and pressed them against her forehead.

"It can't be that bad, can it?" asked Jill.

"Yes, Jill, it can. And I'm sick over it. Sick with shame." Thin tears slid slowly down her face. "Jill, I can't pay my bills."

Visions of everything from unpaid funeral charges to salivating loan sharks ran through Jill's mind. How could this be happening to a resident of Cinnamon Key? To one of her residents? If not wealthy, most of these people were quite comfortable in their retirements. Jill pulled a napkin from the dispenser and handed it to her. "How long has this been going on?"

Barbara sniffed and blotted her cheeks. "Things have been difficult ever since Raymond died."

"But, surely, Raymond left you insurance."

"A minimum, Jill. Except for the certificates of deposit, all I have is my Social Security. Once Raymond gave up his medical practice, he discovered the dog track and couldn't control himself. He gambled away everything." The older woman closed her eyes. "He took out loans that he never told me about."

"I understand," Jill said. And she did. Her own father had done exactly the same thing, leaving her mother and his children practically destitute. The ugly episode had changed Jill's life forever. "What about your children, Barbara? Can't they help you?" she asked, remembering how she helped her family.

"I can't ask them. They have bills of their own. And they thought the world of their father." She managed a small smile. "One of my CDs will mature later next month and then I'll be fine."

"Can't you cash it in early and pay the penalty? If you compare the interest you're paying at Dilby's—"

"I thought about doing that but, after everything I've been through, Jill, I realized I couldn't take any more humiliation. I kept imagining the pitying stares from people at the bank when they figured out the truth. And everyone gossips. Once the story got back to Cinnamon Key, I would have died of embarrassment."

"I see," Jill said gently. "Barbara, Raymond's been gone for eight months. Have you been pawning your possessions all that time?"

"Just for the last three months."

Three months. A warning prickle started up Jill's spine as the older woman continued.

"Dilby's holding several of my things, including that little painting we bought years ago in Spain." Smiling, she opened and closed the earpieces on her sunglasses. "You know, Ralph Webster always admired that painting. He noticed it wasn't on the wall and was asking about it last week." Her voice began thickening. "I told him I thought I'd put it away somewhere. He's such a kind man. He stops by just to see how I'm doing." Raising her chin, she gulped back tears. "You know, I couldn't tell him the truth about my financial situation. I have my pride."

Jill paused before she continued. "Do you think Ralph noticed any other items were gone from your house?"

Barbara stared off into space before she answered. "Come to think of it, yes. Yes, I do. For one, he asked me about the jade figurines in my china cabinet. I suppose it was foolish of me, but I was in such a dither over his question, I told him I couldn't remember any jade figurines in my china cabinet. I guess he thinks I'm still a mess over Raymond's death."

Jill covered her forehead with her hand. "Oh, my goodness," she mumbled. "That's got to be the explanation."

"For what?"

"Remember I told you Ralph's nephew was visiting?"

"Oh, yes. Little Andy."

"Drew. He said Ralph suspects one of his neighbors is being robbed. Barbara, he must think you're the one being robbed." Relief enveloped her like a cool breeze. She opened her hands toward Barbara. "I knew there had to be an explanation. How could anyone think Cinnamon Key was being burglarized? Now I can tell him—"

Barbara Brody came halfway out of her seat, her eyes bright with fear. "No! You can't do that."

Jill grabbed for her arms. "I'm so sorry. Of course I won't."

"People talk, Jill. I couldn't deal with pity. And I swear, this will all be over next month when that first CD matures." Her tears started again as she stared at the tabletop. "My children and grandchildren live in California. My husband's dead. All I have left is Max and my life here at Cinnamon Key."

Jill hadn't figured out how she was going to handle the situation with Drew, but right now Barbara Brody was verging on hysteria. "It's okay. Really. Your secret is safe with me, Barbara."

Wiping her eyes, Barbara whispered, "What about Ralph Webster thinking I'm so upset that I don't even know I'm being robbed? Do you think he'll tell any of my other neighbors?"

"I don't think Ralph Webster's the problem, Barbara."

Barbara sat back in the booth and nibbled her lip. "Oh, dear. It's little Andy, isn't it? What are we going to do about him?"

Jill leaned her elbows on the red Formica table. "Just tell me everything you've pawned, and we'll figure out a story in case Ralph or anyone else asks. And don't worry, Barbara. I'll take care of little Andy."

Two days later Jill was folding clothes in the laundry room at the back of the clubhouse. The machines were an emergency backup for the residents, and she was glad she'd fought to have them installed. She made it a point to do an occasional load of laundry at the facility because it gave her an additional opportunity to talk with the residents.

"So this is what you do on your day off," Drew said in a loud whisper.

She was shaking out a sheet, and at the sound of his voice Jill froze. She held her breath; he was inches behind her. The ballooning flower-printed material hung in the air, then deflated, before she remembered to breathe again.

Drew caught a corner of the sheet before it touched the floor. Gathering the material into his arms, he bunched it between them. Was it that his face was so close to hers, she wondered, or that it was appearing above her bed sheet, that had her so flustered? Or was it simply seeing him again after a two-day absence?

"Wh-what did you say to me?"

He smiled slowly, then buried his nose in the freshly washed material and inhaled. "Who cares? Your sheets smell terrific."

Before she had a chance to react, he lifted his face and grinned. "Here, let me help you fold." Fishing out two corners, he backed up to the table.

She chewed the inside of her cheek while she waited for those warm vibrations between her neck and knees to subside. When it became apparent they weren't going to stop, she decided on the next-best thing. She'd pretend he wasn't having an effect on her.

"Thanks," she said cheerfully. When he continued his teasing grin, she decided to try for less cheer and more dignity. Not an easy thing to accomplish, considering she was dressed for the poolside with nothing but a gauzy tunic over her swimsuit. His beige linen blazer and trousers might have appeared smartly casual in other circumstances. In the confines of the laundry room, and dressed the way she was, he looked downright intimidating. She fixed her gaze on the sheet. "I stopped by Ralph's yesterday, but no one was home." She made a vertical fold in the sheet. "I thought you might have gone back to New Jersey."

"And not come to say good-bye to you? Perish the thought." He brought his corners together, and she followed, making another vertical fold. "Uncle Ralph asked me to go to Miami with him yesterday morning. The shop called and said his car was ready. I stopped by to tell you I was going, but the sign on your door said you were out." Lifting the sheet to the side, he gave her a better view of his clothes. "I did some necessary shopping, and we talked about the burglaries." Walking forward, Drew handed his corners to her. "I thought you'd like to know what I've found out."

"Oh, that again," she said breezily.

Picking up the bottom end, he lifted the corners to her hands and held them there for several seconds. "Yes, that again. Her name's Barbara Brody. She's been recently widowed and—"

She let him take the sheet from her grasp. "So Ralph thinks Barbara's being robbed."

"My uncle is convinced of it." Drew listed the pawned items with chilling accuracy as he completed folding the sheet. "That all adds up to several thousand dollars' worth of fenceable merchandise."

At that moment an older gentleman pushed through the door with a basket of clothes in his arms. He dumped the load plus two heaping scoops of soap powder into a machine. Shoving coins into the coin slots, he hit the Start button, then walked up to Jill. "I'll be back to check on those clothes later, Jill."

Wincing at the amount of soap powder he'd used, she looked up at Drew. "I'll keep an eye on them. Ben, this is Ralph Webster's nephew, Drew. Drew, Ben Winger. He edits the community newsletter." While the two men shook hands, she reviewed her prepared response for Drew. When Ben Winger was out of earshot, she folded her arms and leaned against a dryer. "All of those supposedly missing items of Barbara's sound like heirlooms. Did you ever stop to think she's sent them on to her children out in California and has put the things out of her mind?"

"She didn't tell that to Uncle Ralph. When he's brought things up to her, she's given vague answers, as if she isn't the least concerned. He says she's had a difficult time adjusting to widowhood, but how can she forget what she did with her piano?"

Piano? Jill felt a cold ball of panic land in the center of her stomach. Barbara hadn't mentioned selling her piano.

"Did you hear what I just said, Jill?"

"Uh, yes. Yes, I did." She turned around to peer into the dryer. Lying to Drew was bad enough, but looking him in the eye while she was concocting a fib was impossible. Holding on to the round glass door, she grabbed at the first thought that came by. "If I remember correctly, Mr. Brody played the piano, not Barbara. And, anyway, someone in the neighborhood would have noticed a piano being taken."

Drew's eyebrows went up, but she rambled on nervously. "Barbara probably had the thing carted off to the Salvation Army." Sneaking another peek at Drew, she saw his brow wrinkling with doubt, then cursed herself for the cavalier tone of her explanation. What if Barbara had sold the piano? A thing like that was easily traced, and he was too smart to let the remark go by. He stared her straight in the eye.

"Salvation Army? Maybe. Maybe not." Indicating the dryer with a jut of his chin, he moved closer. "Anything else in there?"

She was no good at lying and never would be. And why was he still holding her bed sheet . . . smoothing her bed sheet so sensuously with his fingers . . . warming her bed sheet so invitingly with his hands? She pressed her lips together in an attempt to calm herself. Turning from him, she stuck her head in the open dryer. Her pillowcases were the last two things in there. Way in there. And he wasn't going to touch them.

"We'll ask Mrs. Brody about the piano tonight," he added.

Tonight? She hadn't had the opportunity to speak to Ralph yet, and they were planning to bring this up with Barbara tonight! The poor woman was having a difficult time holding her emotions together with only Jill around. What was going to happen when the Webster men got a shot at her? Jill pulled back from the dryer so fast, she banged her head. "Ow!"

"Are you okay?"

"Yes, I'm okay." So much for maintaining dignity, she thought, as she rubbed the top of her head. "What about tonight?"

"We're having you and Mrs. Brody over for dinner." He leaned against the folding table to make room for two women to pass. "Good afternoon, ladies."

Both nodded, and one turned to Jill. "A wheel on that laundry cart has come completely off. We can't jam it back on. Should we report it to maintenance?"

Before Jill could speak, Drew did. "I'll take a look at it, ladies."

"Thank you," said one as they headed for the door.

"Drew, you don't have to—"

He held up his hand as he fought back a smile. "I know, I know. You can take care of it."

"Yes."

Crossing his arms over the folded sheet, he held it against his chest and began rubbing the material with his thumbs. Her nipples tightened as she watched the subtle but thorough way he manipulated the corners. There was a deliberateness to his movement that made her mouth go dry. The next thing she knew, she was picturing herself writhing on that same bed sheet as he used his thumbs in the same accurate way on her.

"You shouldn't be concerning yourself with broken laundry carts. Today is your day off."

Her heart fluttered like the wings of a baby bird trying to fly. And then she felt it thump to an undignified landing at the bottom of her rib cage. She'd been staring at his thumbs, totally involved in a torrid fantasy, when the reality of his words hit with a bang. "How did you know this is my day off?"

"I made some inquiries."

Disquieted by his answer, she parted her lips and cocked her chin. "You were asking about me?"

"I was discreet. By the way, we're having Cuban food tonight. In fact, Uncle Ralph is in his kitchen right now making flan. Mrs. Brody's already accepted our invitation. Can we count on you?"

Of course they could count on her. How could she possibly say no? Both men would want to question Barbara, and Jill wasn't going to let the emotionally fragile woman face them alone. Even if one of them was a caring neighbor and the other was so . . . She looked up at Drew. So unbelievably handsome. They were alone in the noisy room. He was moving closer. She wasn't moving anywhere except back to that torrid fantasy on her sheets. He whispered her name, and then all hell broke loose.

A soapy waterfall suddenly cascaded over the top of a washer and was splashing onto the floor and over their feet. The machine shook violently as a loud buzzer began blasting nonstop.

"Ben Winger overloaded. Quick, hit the Stop button," she shouted, as she reached for it herself. During the slippery scuffle to remain standing, she grabbed Drew around the waist.

"Missed," he said, before they both went down, clinging to each other in a wave of gurgling suds. Landing on his side, he curled his arm to break her fall. Hip to hip, chest to breasts, they couldn't have been closer unless they'd been naked. When they'd caught their breath, she began a slippery struggle to put space between them. Her gauzy cover-up was plastered around her middle, allowing plenty of slick skin contact with the vinyl floor. The harder she tried to disentangle herself from his embrace, the more her pelvis did a horizontal bump and grind against his hip.

"Let me help you, or you'll slip again."

"I've got to turn off the machine." She made it up on one knee before sliding on top of him. Her face was inches from his and scarlet. The soapy river continued in thickening swirls around his shoulders. Pushing frantically off him again, she almost made it to her feet but slipped, landing astride his hips this time. Soapsuds dripped from her one ear. "What if someone finds us like this?"

He was laughing too hard to answer.

"Drew, do you have any idea how this must look?" she whispered desperately.

When he caught his breath, he lifted up on both elbows. "Like Deborah Kerr and Burt Lancaster on the beach?"

"Drew!"

"You're right," he said, twisting her onto her back and locking his knee over hers. "I think Burt was on top. Don't you?"

"I think this is more in line with *I Love Lucy*," she said through several grunts. Bumping her hips against his in an attempt to move out from under him, she tried a polite "Just get off me, please."

He tried. He really tried, but her provocative movements sent them several inches across the floor. When they hit the bank of dryers, his hips had sunk fully between her thighs. "Oops." He was fighting to maintain a serious expression, but there was nothing he could do about the silent laughter now shaking his body.

"It's not funny," she said, slapping him on the shoulder. But it was. As the sudsy water continued eddying around them with alarming speed, she bit her lip to keep from laughing. "It isn't," she insisted defiantly. When he raised his head to look at her, his teasing expression melted her resolve.

"Jill," he whispered, shifting his hips against her welcoming hold.

"Oh, Drew." Before she could think to stop him, his mouth was covering hers in a breath-stealing kiss. The surreal sensations of swirling water, the irritating buzzer, and his erection throbbing between her legs were sending all reason from her mind. When she dragged one knee up his thigh, he groaned and deepened their kiss. The delicious tension between her legs tightened to a pulsing pleasure. Pressing her hands against the small of his spine, she drew her other knee up to his hip. He slid his hand beneath her bottom, urging her to move against him. She did, and the rest of the universe whirled around them in lemon-scented clouds and protesting sounds. But nothing mattered except the solid feel of the man she cradled with her body. Absolutely nothing.

Then the buzzer stopped.

She slowly opened her eyes. Lifting his lips from hers, Drew looked around the laundry room as if it were Mars. The washing machine slowly stopped its bubbling cascade, and the river around them changed directions, heading toward the drain near their feet. Drew's wandering gaze returned to her.

"Please get off me."

"Right," he said, rolling off her and sitting up. He helped her into a sitting position. "Are you okay?"

"I'll live if you promise me you'll never speak of this," she managed, her cheeks stinging with embarrassing heat.

"Would it be okay if I think about it now and then?"

Her glance flicked sideways to take in his deadpan expression. "Not another word," she warned.

They were both brushing off the suds when the door opened. Ben Winger took one step inside and stopped. The man's embarrassment was evident in his sheepish grin. "Used a bit too much soap powder, did I?"

"Just a little," Jill replied with as much dignity as she could muster over Drew's laughter.

FOUR

"I can do this." Reaching out to ring Ralph Webster's doorbell, Jill whispered the words again, embracing them like a mantra. Even though she hadn't gotten to talk with Barbara about the piano, this evening was going to be a manageable one. She would see to that.

"Honest," she mumbled, trying bravely to ignore the panicky quivers in her belly. Tapping her nails against her belt, she reviewed her situation while she waited. The laundry room was back in order and, more important, so was her list of priorities.

At the top of the list was handling Drew. Ringing the bell again, she amended the thought. She was not going to handle him, she was not going to touch him, she was not getting close to him at all. And she certainly was not going to think about what happened on the floor of the laundry room.

"I can do this. I can do this," she chanted softly as the door swung open.

She'd expected to see Ralph. Instead, she was looking at the man who inspired visible signs of neurosis in her. Tall, tempting, and oh-so-touchable Drew Webster leaned forward.

"Dried off nicely after our bubble bath, I see."

She should have chanted longer. Too late now. With his loaded compliment her inner calm disintegrated, and her thoughts were jolted back to the laundry room. For a few pulsating moments she'd allowed him to roll around the floor with her, kissing her, touching her.

She looked away from him. Allowed him? Heck, no. She'd cradled his hard, masculine body in her slippery, wet embrace, encouraging the lusty encounter. The heat suffusing her body began concentrating in her face.

"For me?" Drew asked, pointing to the bird-of-paradise flowers in the crook of her arm.

She stared down at the orange and cobalt-blue blossoms as if she were seeing them for the first time. "What? Oh, these are for Ralph."

"Well, I'm disappointed, Jill." Stepping out onto the porch, he peeled back the waxy green paper wrapped around the stalks. "I thought these might have been an apology."

"For what?"

"Knocking me down today."

Stealing a glance at him through her lowered lashes, she found him staring back with his "gotcha" grin. Stinging heat enveloped her ears, leading her to wonder if spontaneous combustion were possible. He wasn't going to let the incident rest. The scamp. Of course, if she had to be honest, there had been an element of humor involved. Before she lost a tug-of-war over her own emerging smile, Ralph appeared in the doorway.

"Let her in, Drew. She looks as if she's about to have heatstroke."

Ralph's thinning gray hair was combed neatly back from his face, his blue shirt matched his eyes, and when he planted a kiss on her cheek, she could smell his Old Spice. His hearty greeting took her mind off Drew.

"Isn't Barbara with you?"

Something about the way he was leaning out the door for a glimpse of Barbara struck Jill as odd. Studying Ralph, she felt her eyes narrowing with curiosity. Surely, Ralph wasn't fearful for the woman's safety when there was still light in the sky and he could see her house from his front door. More than likely his "little Andy" had him on guard. Whatever the explanation, she was thankful her face and ears were cooling down.

"I stopped by to pick her up, Ralph, but she's probably out walking Max." Following Drew inside, she inhaled deeply. "What in heaven's name smells so good?"

"The balsamic vinegar in the black beans. Barbara likes that," he said, straining for one last look before closing the door.

"Everything's fine over there, Ralph," she said. And then a thought began forming in her mind. She'd had so much on her mind lately, had she missed the obvious? Was it possible that Ralph Webster had more than a neighborly interest in Barbara? Was there a new romance in the air at Cinnamon Key?

"Thank you for the flowers, Jill." He turned to his nephew. "Aren't these some beauties she brought us?"

The phone rang as Drew turned his one palm upward and shrugged. "She didn't bring them for me."

Ralph's gaze shifted from Drew to Jill, then back to Drew. "That must be my stockbroker. Be a good houseboy, Andy," he said, slapping the flowers into his hand. "Put these in water while I answer the phone. You'll find a vase in the kitchen." Heading down the hall, he warned, "And don't do anything to make Jill blush again."

"What about her?" he called to his uncle. Holding the flowers against his chest, he looked at Jill. "What if she makes me blush again?"

Scenes from her struggle on the laundry-room floor burst, slick and wet, into her consciousness again. The bumps and grinds, the slippery landings, and all of those lusty sensations came flooding back to her. By that devilish look in his eyes, she knew he was reading her thoughts and prompting more of the same. She had to change the subject or die trying.

"I'm sorry I'm late but—"

"You're not." He took a step toward her.

She pointed at the flowers. "Shouldn't we—?"

"In a moment." He took another step.

She looked around his shoulder. "Maybe we should stir the—?"

"Maybe we should." He lowered his head toward hers.

Her lips began tingling, and her breath was nowhere to be found. She flattened herself against the wall.

Bracing one hand on the door, he nuzzled his nose against hers. When she didn't resist, he shifted closer, pressing his thighs against hers. Those same determined thighs that had fit so satisfyingly between her own. For one insane moment she closed her eyes, allowing her body to remember and respond. Pulsing heat gathered between her legs as he caressed her buttock with a slow hand.

"I like your outfit. You remind me of a candy cane in those red stripes. Good enough to lick."

Every time they were alone, every time he came near her, her brain went soft, and she started melting. "Drew. If we keep on like this . . ." She meant to hold his face steady between her hands to tell him . . . something. She'd think of that in a moment. Right now her mouth was busy urging his open. He wasn't cooperating; he was teasing her with hit-and-run kisses all over her face. Running her hands over his shoulders, she breathed in little gulps of air. "Drew, someone could come."

"What a delightful thought," he whispered against her mouth.

"I didn't mean . . ." she began, then quickly slid sideways out of his embrace. Distancing herself from him by several feet, she shoved her fingers through her hair. "Where does Ralph keep his vases?" she asked, her voice all business. "Under the sink? I keep mine under the sink." Grabbing the flowers from him, she headed into the kitchen but stopped short of shutting the door behind her.

Before she could control the situation, she had to get control herself. And that didn't mean running away. This was his uncle's house, but this was her world, and even though he'd insisted on invading it, she was still in charge. Pulling the waxy paper from around the stalks, she waved him in with it. "Let's get these flowers in water before they start wilting."

"Wilting. That would be a shame," he said, passing her on the way to the sink, "because I hate it when anything wilts from neglect." Opening the bottom cabinet, he bent over to search.

He had the cutest butt she'd ever seen, compact and perfectly proportioned for his broad shoulders and trim waist. He could have been a male underwear model. She pressed her fingertips between her eyes and waited for the second wave of temporary insanity to pass. The kissing, flirting, and butt admiring had to stop if she was going to get through this evening.

Drew backed out from beneath the sink with an empty olive-oil can in his hands. "This should do," he said, placing the can on the counter. "Let's see those." Taking the flowers from her, he looked them over. Without warning he pulled a knife from the knife block and deftly chopped through the lower ends of the stalks. They made a plunking sound as they hit the sink. Before Jill could intervene, he'd whacked off several more inches. Glancing at her, he laid them aside and ran water in the can. "You look horrified."

"Do you always do things that way?"

"What way?" Inserting the flowers in the container, he arranged them in a fan.

"You didn't measure to see how much to cut off. You just," she said, gesturing with her one hand, "chopped."

Keeping his eyes on the flowers, he stuck out his lower lip and nodded. "When I'm pretty certain of how things will turn out, yes, I do things that way."

If his actions were indicative of his usual behavior, she was in more trouble than she'd thought. Drew Webster played by his own rules, and nothing she could say would change that fact. Once he decided on something, she concluded miserably, his passionate nature would be next to impossible to restrain. She felt a frown forming on her face but didn't bother to stop it.

"Well?" he asked with comical impatience.

She conceded the obvious. "They look fabulous."

He dumped the cut stalks into the trash under the sink, then rested his weight on the cabinet door. "So do you."

The kitchen grew smaller as the pull between them increased. Somewhere in the back of the house mambo music started and stopped several times. He didn't close in on her this time. It didn't matter. Nothing did except the truth reflected in his eyes. And she was going to fight it. "This thing between us, it's all about sex," she blurted out.

"No, it's not."

The staring match continued until Jill bowed her head and walked over to the stove. Lifting a lid, she picked up a spoon and stirred the beans with the determination of a hungry camper. Before she spoke, she added another item to her list of priorities. No more eye contact with him.

"Drew, we should be talking about this burglary business."

"We will. Tonight we're going to get to the bottom of it," he said, peeling a banana and dropping it into the blender.

"You're not going to bombard Barbara with a lot of questions, are you? She's still getting used to living on her own." Rapping the spoon against the pot's edge, she set it in the spoon rest.

"Bull."

"What?" She replaced the lid with a clatter. "What do you mean, bull?"

"I mean what I said—we have to get to the bottom of this. Sooner or later some basic facts will have to be established. Why not here, with her friends around her?" Leaning his hip against the sink, he poured the rum straight from the bottle into the blender. "Why not tonight?"

He was doing it again. Tricking her with his one-step-ahead-of-everyone mind. Where was that control she'd thought she'd regained? "You can't fling a word like 'burglary' around a sixty-eight-year-old woman living alone for the first time in her life. You have to be sensitive."

"And I'm not sensitive?"

"I'm not saying that. I—" Her words were cut short by the doorbell. Then she heard the door open, several sharp barks, and a familiar voice.

"Yoo-hoo. Anyone home?"

Max's toenails were already clicking on the foyer tiles as Jill picked up the can of flowers. She had to talk to Barbara before Drew, sensitive or not, pounced on her with his questions. Holding her hand up like a traffic cop, she began backing out of the room. "Stay there and finish what you're doing. I'll put these in the dining room." Before she could exhale, Max skittered around the corner, tumbled onto his side, and slid into the kitchen. Scrambling onto all fours and yapping wildly, he made a second break for Drew's pant leg, where he attached himself like a piece of lint.

"There you are," she said, hurrying out before Barbara could enter. As soon as she'd closed the door to the kitchen, she took Barbara by the hand and led her away from it. "Drew's in there," she explained over the whine of the blender.

"Little Andy?" Barbara asked brightly.

"Yes. And he's going to ask you what happened to your piano. He said Ralph didn't get a straight answer from you. Where is it?"

"I sold the piano," she said, with apology evident in her exaggerated whisper. "I didn't intend to hide the fact from Ralph, but something happened when he asked me about it."

"What happened? Was Ralph badgering you?"

Coiling the dog leash in her hands, Barbara shook her head. "I—I don't know how to explain it, Jill. Ralph was standing so close to me, and he took my hand, and, well . . . I just became so flustered. The next thing I knew, I was telling him that I couldn't remember what I'd done with that darn piano. I couldn't think straight."

"Barbara," she said gently, "do you think you're up to this dinner tonight?"

The older woman leveled a disbelieving stare at Jill. "For heaven's sakes, of course I am. And I already know what I'm going to tell them. I'll say the piano was a constant reminder of my late husband. And then I'll say I felt uncomfortable talking about selling Raymond's favorite possession."

Embracing the can of flowers, Jill felt a weight lifting from her shoulders. "Barbara, that's a perfect explanation. And when he brings up the rest of the things, you just stick to that story we came up with about sending them all to your children." Decidedly calmer now, she gave the older woman a hug. "There aren't any more surprises you haven't told me about, right?"

Pressing her lips together, Barbara looked away and sighed. Her confidence appeared to be crumbling. She rubbed a thumb over the metal fastener on the leash.

Jill closed her eyes. She didn't like the feeling of where this was going. "Barbara, is there something you haven't told me? Something else I should know about?"

"Raymond had a bookie."

Before Jill could close her mouth, Drew pushed through the kitchen door with Max dangling from his pant leg.

"Max, you naughty dog. Let go of him this instant," Barbara said.

The dog released his grip, sat back, and wagged his tail.

"So those are the magic words. I tried waving

beefsteak in front of him, and he still wouldn't budge for me." Reaching out his hand to Barbara, he smiled. "Hello, I'm Drew Webster."

"I'm Barbara Brody."

And I'm in shock, thought Jill. Raymond had a bookie? Her imagination ran wild with the possible implications. Dr. Raymond Brody, the man who wrote such a glowing letter of reference for her brother's application to medical school, had a bookie? On the periphery of her consciousness, she heard Drew saying something about Max. Nothing registered through her panic until Drew reached down to scratch Max behind the ears.

"With his tenacity he has the makings of a great guard dog for you."

"A guard dog? In Cinnamon Key? Whatever for?" Barbara asked.

So this was his segue to a discussion on burglary. And they hadn't even moved out of the foyer. Before he could continue, Jill closed her hand around his elbow and hauled him up. "Didn't I hear the blender before? Is anyone thirsty?"

"I almost forgot. We'll have liquid instead of frozen daiquiris if I don't serve them soon. Why don't you go on into the living room. I'll be right in with them."

As soon as the kitchen door closed, Jill

turned to Barbara. "Your husband had a bookie? Is this man threatening you?"

The older woman stared at Max. "I know I should have told you, but I was more ashamed of Raymond's bookie than anything else. He called me yesterday to tell me he'd appreciate another payment—"

"Another payment?"

Barbara nodded as Jill hurried her into the far corner of the living room. "Raymond ran up quite a bill. I got in touch with a piano store in Naples. They came right over and picked up the baby grand. They gave me cash for it, and I went out today to pay Hector."

"Hector," repeated Jill.

"The bookie." She looked at Jill. "Oh, I'm so sorry, Jill. I've upset you, haven't I?"

The tone of concern in Barbara's voice and the stricken look on her face had Jill struggling to control her uneasiness. There was no reason to make this evening more difficult for Barbara than it was already going to be. "I'm not upset. I want you to be happy and safe. I guess I've seen too many movies with nasty bookies. What's this Hector like?"

"Hector does not have a heart of gold, but he's not threatening to break my kneecaps either. He just wants his money."

Broken kneecaps? Jill grabbed Barbara's hand.

"Promise me you won't see Hector again unless I'm with you."

"But, Jill, I—"

"Hello, Barbara."

Barbara turned at the sound of Ralph's voice. "Hello, Ralph," she said softly.

Jill stood aside as the two walked to each other in the middle of the room.

"You look lovely in that shade of pink, Barbara."

"Thank you. And thank you for having me to dinner."

Surer than ever about the budding romance, Jill quietly placed the flowers on the coffee table and made her way toward the kitchen door. She'd almost ensured them a few minutes of privacy until Max, pacing by the glass doors, began growling.

"Hush, Max," Barbara said. As Drew came into the room with a tray of banana daiquiris, she continued, "He's been doing that a lot lately. Growling at his reflection."

"Are you sure it's his reflection he's been growling at?" Drew asked, offering a drink to Jill.

"What kind of question is that?" Swiping a glass from the tray, Jill gave him a stern look of warning.

"You don't smile enough," he said under his breath.

"Yes," Ralph added, "what kind of question is that?"

Drew crossed the room to where Barbara and his uncle were standing. As they took their drinks, Drew continued, "Just a question. Like, whatever happened to that Spanish painting my uncle mentioned you had? He said he'd missed seeing it the last time he dropped by your place."

"The Spanish painting," repeated Barbara.

Max began growling again.

Barbara's attention bounced off Max to Drew, and then Ralph.

"The Spanish painting." The cocktail napkin dropped from her fingers. "I . . . stop that, Max. I . . . I. Max, stop that pawing." She looked helplessly toward Jill. "I forgot what I was going to say."

"I believe you mentioned sending some things to your children. In California." Jill nodded deeply, urging Barbara to agree.

"Uh. Yes, yes, that's what I did with . . . those things."

Shifting into a maniacal frenzy, Max went up on his hind legs against the glass.

Taking a step closer to Ralph, Barbara asked, "Do you think there is someone out there?"

"We're fine," said Ralph, reaching out to touch the older woman's sleeve.

Drew coughed. "Speaking of missing things,

Barbara, whatever happened to that piano of yours?" Taking a sip of his drink, Drew lowered the empty tray to his side and waited for her reply.

Silence ballooned rapidly as all eyes turned to Barbara. Ignoring the prickles dancing along her spine, Jill offered Barbara a confident raise of her eyebrows, but it was already too late. The older woman was suddenly the focus of unwanted attention. While scowling at Drew, Jill stole a glance at Barbara. By the confusion on the older woman's face, Jill realized Barbara thought the disapproving look was meant for her. Making matters worse, Max threw himself into another fit of barking, startling everyone this time.

Ralph handed his drink to Barbara and headed toward the kitchen, crooking his finger at Drew when he neared the door. "Can I see you a minute?"

"Now?"

"Now," he said, holding open the kitchen door.

"You see, Barbara," Drew heard Jill say, as he walked into the kitchen, "he's only barking at Ralph's ceramic elephants. Out there in the garden by that Brazilian pepper tree."

When his uncle took his drink and the tray and placed them soundly on the counter, Drew knew he was in trouble. Take-it-in-the-ear trouble.

"I haven't been so upset with you since you lost that camel outside of Cairo back in 1973. At least then I could send you to bed without dessert."

"Nineteen Seventy-four. What have I done?"

"You've been inconsiderate to a lady."

"I was just asking a few questions. What's wrong with that?"

Ralph shook his head. "I knew I should never have mentioned the word 'burglary' to you. You always were obsessive about unraveling those mystery novels."

"Uncle, this isn't a mystery novel." Both men turned around as Jill entered the kitchen. "And before *you* start in on me, I was, too, being sensitive."

"As sensitive as a bulldozer going downhill," she shot back, after pulling the door closed behind her.

"Where's Barbara?" Ralph asked.

"She's taken Max outside to sniff the elephants." She turned to Drew. "You promised you wouldn't upset her. Can't you see she's getting upset?"

"Yes," chimed in Ralph. "Would you lay off the burglary business? Barbara's explained where her painting and things are, and I don't care about her piano if she doesn't. So knock off the questions. We're not playing Clue here."

Drew raised his hands in momentary defeat. "Sorry. Not another word about it." When his uncle and Jill headed for the door, he added, "At least not tonight. I swear, the two of you won't know I'm checking on a thing. I'll be the invisible man."

His uncle opened his arms to the ceiling. Speaking to Jill, he said, "He's always had an active imagination. I already told him, I'm convinced I was mistaken about there being any burglaries at Barbara's, but he won't listen to me. You talk to him, Jill." Pushing open the door, he added, "Maybe he'll listen to you."

Jill's shoulders dropped several noticeable inches as she turned on her heel to face him. "Your uncle told you that he doesn't think there are any burglaries going on. Barbara certainly doesn't think there are any. And I'm in complete agreement with the both of them. You're hanging on to this like Max on a pant leg. Why?"

"Why didn't she tell my uncle where her things had gotten to when he first asked her? Something is not right."

"What's not right is you upsetting Barbara. And your uncle. Not to mention the possibility of upsetting the neighborhood if you don't drop this. So you ought to drop this. Direct your energies to enjoying this visit with Ralph." She squinted at him. "What's that look for?"

"You're in an awful hurry to smooth this over."

"Of course I am, because there's nothing to it. Why should I stand by and see my friends upset for nothing?"

"Is that your only reason?" He reached for his drink, watching her closely.

"My job is more than sales. I'm the liaison between the developers and the residents. When there's a problem, I'm expected to handle it. If Merriweather Development starts receiving letters from frightened residents, the home office is going to want to know what's going on here. And there's nothing going on here. Period."

"Jill, it's none of my business—"

Anger flashed in her blue-green eyes. "You said it."

And he was going to say more. "But you pay an awful lot of attention to the private lives of these residents. Maybe too much."

"Do you want to know what I think?"

"Passionately," he teased, hoping to defuse her emotion. Ignoring his attempt, she pushed full steam ahead.

"I think your priorities are screwed up, Drew. You fly around the country taking care of your business, and then, when you manage to squeeze in a week for your uncle, you waste precious time chasing after phantom criminals. Drew, he's not getting any younger."

The part about phantom criminals was still up for discussion, but she was right about the rest. No matter how vigorous and engaged in life his uncle was, Ralph Webster wasn't getting any younger. A weekly phone call and a short visit couldn't begin to show his uncle how grateful he was for everything Ralph had done for him. He held Jill's gaze for a long while. Long enough to feel an inner clock beginning to reset itself. Long enough to know he was going to like the elegant new cadence. Long enough to know that Jill Stuart was good for him and that he was good for her. "Thank you."

"For what?" she asked, looking apprehensive.

"For being honest with me when I needed it. Webster's Landscaping can get along without me for a while." He moved closer to her, whispering close to her ear. "I have *beaucoup* unfinished business here, Jill." Her lips parted as she began lowering her lashes. Pressing closer to her, he reveled in her sensual response.

"What kind of unfinished business?" she managed, swallowing with difficulty.

"Mostly personal." Moving aside the curvy lock of hair he'd been playing with, he began kissing the top of her ear. When he began licking it, she shivered, leaning into the sensation with a sigh.

"You mean . . . proving to your uncle how . . . ahhhh . . . important he is to you?"

"That's part of it."

"What else, Drew?" Before he answered, she seemed to struggle up from some depths. Pushing him back, she faced him with nostrils flaring. "Not this burglary stuff."

He took a step, then another. Forcing her to walk backward, he stopped when she bumped into the counter. "You said you didn't want to hear anything more on that subject."

"Th-that's right."

"But you'd like to know what else I've got planned, wouldn't you?" Lowering his face closer to hers, he repeated in a whisper, "Wouldn't you?"

Her eyes fluttered shut as she raised her mouth. "Wouldn't I what?" she asked, moistening her lips.

"Like to know what else I'm planning."

Her lips formed a silent response. "Like what?"

"Like proving to you this thing between us is more than just a sexual attraction." Leaving her leaning backward and unkissed at the counter, he turned and headed for the living room. "Now what the hell could Barbara have done with that piano?"

As he pushed through the door, he could hear Jill racing to catch up with him, whispering something that sounded like, "I can do this."

FIVE

"Imagine meeting you here."

Jill's heart was already drumming against her rib cage by the time she'd stood up from her beach chair and turned around. Walking out of the Australian pines and oleander, Drew was making his way straight for her across the shell-strewn sand. His cranberry T-shirt and white shorts, plastered against him in a warm gust of air, were accentuating every masculine line and ridge on his body. The sight started her built-in warning system buzzing, and she stepped back into ankle-deep surf. He kept on coming, cursing under his breath as he did a crazy barefoot dance past the palms and across broken bits of shells.

Fighting her own painful smile, she slipped her itching hands and clenched fingers behind her back, then jerked them to her side, reprimanding herself. Since Ralph's dinner she'd succeeded in keeping tabs on Drew without ending up alone with him. Now he had her cornered, and she was being rocketed with the urge to hug him—and the urge to scold him. She wasn't sure which was stronger. What was wrong with her? She was tingling with anticipation as her heart tripped into double time.

Careful, she warned herself. No matter what Drew had said, their biggest attraction for each other was physical. For all she knew about him, which wasn't much, he could have a lover waiting for him in New Jersey. He was fun, and he did love his uncle, but if she was to get involved with someone, he would have to be someone she could depend on. Oddly enough, though, she sensed Drew was the type she could depend on. Almost. She rolled her eyes. Falling into a false sense of security went against her nature, didn't it? Even after dinner when Barbara explained about selling her piano, Drew still hadn't said he'd given up his preposterous theory of burglaries. She eyed him with open suspicion when he stopped a few steps short of her.

"Did you follow me?" she asked.

A hurt look briefly crossed his face. So briefly, she doubted its authenticity.

"I'm running away from home."

"And I'm Huck Finn."

"Okay. My uncle kicked me out."

"I don't believe you."

"Ouch." Steadying himself with a hand on her shoulder, he lifted his foot to pick off a piece of shell. "It's true," he said, removing his hand. "He told me to get a life."

"What? You two have been having a wonderful time together. I saw you laughing up there on the putting green yesterday."

"I love golf. I have an eight handicap, but my uncle swears he'll never play with me again."

"I seriously doubt that," she said, sitting back down in her chair. "Day before yesterday the both of you were smiling when you waved at me." She pointed back through the pines to the residential area. "You were driving out the main gate together towing his fishing boat. Remember?"

"Fishing? I can't believe you brought up fishing," he said, once again turning the conversation to an offshoot subject. "I still let Uncle Ralph bait the hooks. He has this technique that keeps the stuff from leaking out."

Twisting her neck to look up at him, she wrinkled her nose. "Oh, I hate that part, especially when they squirm." Damn. She was playing right into his hands with this silly repartee. Sniffing her disapproval, she started again. "Anyway, how was that ball game last night in Fort

Myers? I know how much Ralph loves base-ball."

"Ah, baseball." Shaking his head, he began dragging his heel in the sand. When he'd made a deep enough depression, he settled his Save the Manatees bag into it. "Speaking of hating things, I hate chewing tobacco at a baseball game. In fact, I hate chewing tobacco, period."

"Well, thanks for sharing that with me. I'll store that information next to my snowplow. Why aren't you with your uncle?"

"According to him, I haven't left him alone for a minute. I'm smothering him with attention. He said I had to get out of the house for the evening or he'd kill me."

Jiggling her beach chair deeper into the sand, she tried to hide her amusement. While he was cuddling closer to her heart, he was also getting closer to convincing her he'd given up his burglary investigation. And if he'd spent every minute with Ralph over the past week, he wouldn't have had the time to snoop around the neighborhood. Right? Maybe. She sighed, rubbing her eyebrows. Maybe not. So why give in when she still wasn't certain? This wasn't the time to ignore her prudent nature. Maybe a few questions and answers would settle things. She frowned. Or stir them up.

Anchoring her gaze to his feet, she smiled at what she saw in spite of her concerns. His tan ended abruptly at his ankles, leaving his feet and toes considerably lighter than the rest of him. There was something engaging, funny, and even vulnerable about pale feet on such a masculine body.

He placed his hands on his knees and leaned down to her eye level. As if he were sharing a secret, he whispered, "Too much golf."

She rolled her tongue along the inside of her cheek, trying not to laugh. Getting giggly over a man's feet was something a teenager might do. Not a grown woman. It simply didn't matter how engaging Drew was, she shouldn't be dwelling on any of his body parts. "So now that little Andy's been kicked out into this harsh Florida winter, what will he do?"

He walked a step or two toward the water and off to the side of where she sat. "Oh, he'll live through it. Little Andy learned his survival techniques years ago." Bending his knees, he lowered himself next to his bag, then dropped his bottom onto the sand. "I think it was that summer in Madrid."

"Madrid?" Glancing at the wine bottle and shiny heel of bread protruding from the bag, she smiled and touched her chin. "You know, I've always wanted to travel to—Well, never mind."

Tugging on the hem of her polka-dot sundress, she pulled it over her knees and looked out toward the horizon. What was she doing? *These feelings—they were all about sex.* They had to be. What else could be the reason behind the sharp, sweet sensations throbbing inside her? And he was being sinfully adorable just to get in her panties. Wasn't he? Squinching up her mouth, she sternly reminded herself that the space inside her, the one marked DREW WEBSTER, would disappear only if she didn't fill it with pieces of him. If she had any sense, she'd get up and leave.

She heard the unmistakable sound of a cork being wrenched from a bottle. "Good. It's still cool," she heard him say.

White Zinfandel. Her favorite. And who the heck had he been with in Madrid? Picking up her notebook, she plopped it into her lap and jerked the pencil out of the spiral.

"Did you want something?" she snapped.

"No, I'm here to enjoy the sunset." Pulling a glass out of the bag, he waved it at her. "Please, go back to what you were doing before I got here. Don't let me interrupt you."

He'd already interrupted her. In fact, he'd been interrupting her for the last fifteen minutes. She'd been planning Nora Plimpton's gazebo wedding, but Drew's face kept getting in the way. It was all because of that silly morning they'd chased Max around the gazebo. Flickering glances in Drew's direction were causing the most incredible images of the two of them in the gazebo . . . alone . . . at night. The tips of her breasts tightened as the images became steamier. With no washing machines or people around, the fantasy surged on. If he touched her right this second . . . Digging a heel in the sand, she crossed one leg tightly over the other.

Forcing her attention back to the page, she doodled furiously in an attempt to get her mind and body to ignore Drew. A chain of tiny triangles appeared on the page, then somehow turned itself into circles and, finally, figure eights. An endless border of figure eights. Tapping the eraser against the design, she looked over at him again. He'd leaned back and was stretching out those long, muscular legs of his. Much too casually. He was up to something. But what was it? And why should she care? Closing her notebook, she twisted around to shove it in the back pocket of her chair. He was getting to her. Right in the neck. Massaging the tight area with one hand, she stared straight out over the Gulf.

"Tense?" When she didn't answer, Drew continued as if she had. "I know. It gets me right here too." He touched his neck and shoulder, the very spot of *her* discomfort.

Go away. Leaning her chin in the cup of her hand, she quietly gritted her teeth and stared at him. *Please go away.* As she continued watching him, she became aware of her mouth relaxing until she was breathing through it. The sinking sun was washing him in a flattering shade of toast, turning an achingly attractive man into a perfect one. And from there he only got better. When a lock of his hair fluttered against his forehead, instead of brushing it away, he closed his eyes, smiling, it seemed, at the sensual feel of it there. Balmy breezes bathed him in more subtle motions, ruffling the short sleeves of his T-shirt and the dark curls covering his forearms, legs, and the small patch visible at the neck of his T-shirt. Lifting her chin a fraction of an inch, she felt her body softening for his touch. There was no overlooking the obvious: His masculinity was stirring the deepest feminine part of her, reminding her of the empty space inside waiting for Drew.

She turned her face toward the horizon, holding on to her obstinacy like a palm in a hurricane. A trick of the slanting rays of the sun, that's why he looked like a gift from the heavens. Right? Another look in his direction blew that theory. No man had ever looked so good. He was smiling at her, his eyes alight with innocence and awareness. And an offering of friendship.

"Can I pour you some?"

A glass of his Zinfandel wouldn't prove a thing; it wouldn't change a thing. She licked the corner of her mouth. She was not getting involved with him. Nodding, she thanked him while telling herself she could handle a few minutes of small talk. Leaning back in the chair, she reached out to take the glass. "So, what were you doing in Madrid?"

"Uncle Ralph was working there and offered to take me in for the summer. You see, shortly after my mother died, my father married a gold digger. I was eleven when my stepmother announced she was divorcing my father. She went after every cent he had in a messy trial." He shook his head with the memory.

As the sky flooded with nameless shades of pink and gold, Jill repositioned herself in his direction. "Ralph's such a helpful person. I'm not at all surprised that he was right there for you. That must have been quite an experience for an eleven-year-old."

Drew dropped his head back and laughed. "It was only the beginning. I discovered there were swarms of money-hungry women in the world, and many of them buzzed around my uncle."

Jill's lips lifted in what she knew was a lame excuse for a smile. She was always uncomfortable talking about money, but hearing what Drew had to say was making her tense. Extremely tense. "I meant the experience of living in a foreign country at such a young age with someone like Ralph."

Propping up a knee, he leaned an elbow in the sand. "Jill, he was more fun than Auntie Mame."

"I'll bet he was," she said, grateful beyond words that they weren't talking about money. "What was it like?"

"He gave me a summer no kid could ever forget. We slept in five different castles."

"Oh, Drew," she said, as her mind spun off images from every fairy tale she'd ever heard. "What a lucky little boy you were."

"That's not the best part. In two of the castles he arranged for us to sleep in the dungeons," he said, with a gleeful enthusiasm that had her laughing out loud. "I had my own horse that summer, too, and I learned to play a mean game of street soccer with the neighborhood kids. By the time September rolled around, I had a pretty respectable handle on my Spanish." Drew looked into his glass, hesitating for a long moment. "My

uncle took care of me when I couldn't take care
of myself. You know how kids are—I had night-
mares of being left alone. I'd wake up in a cold
sweat. He said I'd never be alone as long as he
was alive. We both cried at the airport when I
left." He shook his head. "I love that old man."

The moment grew, like a fragile bubble, big-
ger and more beautiful, until she looked away.
Drew held on to the tenuous silence, sensing
their connection growing stronger. He hadn't
meant to reveal as much about himself as he had,
but he didn't regret telling her any of it. Sipping
his wine, he realized he wanted to tell her more.

"I have a brother in med school," she said,
holding her hair against the breeze. "We're close
too. He just stopped doing that last year. Crying
when we say good-bye, I mean."

Nearby, a flock of orange-beaked gulls skittered back and forth in the surf. Drew broke off
a piece of bread, pitching it their way. "What
about you?" he asked after a while. "Do you cry
at airports?"

Looking down at his toes, she laughed softly. "Yes, but I don't get the hiccups anymore."
Touching that spot on her neck again, she continued, "That's why you're here, isn't it? To
show him how grateful you are."

"And to show him I care. No matter what the
phone companies say, phone calls aren't the best

way to show you care. His living alone causes me some concern."

"Drew, he has a wonderful support system here in Cinnamon Key. You couldn't ask for a better group of neighbors."

"They are a great group," he said, handing her his glass and kneeling behind her chair.

"Who knows? Maybe he'll get married," she said, thinking about the special attention Ralph gave Barbara.

"Never happen," Drew informed her.

"Why are you so certain?"

"He's over seventy, and if he hasn't taken the plunge by now, I don't think he ever will," he said, placing his hands on her neck. "Let me work on that spot for you."

Before she had a chance to protest his offer, he'd started massaging her neck and shoulders. She tensed at his touch, but his slow and gentle pressure eased her rigid posture. Giving in, she slouched against the chair and sighed.

"Tell me about your brother," he said.

"I—I can't talk while you're doing th-this. Tell me more a-about you and Ralph."

"Okay." Feeling her settle into the rhythm of the massage, he began. "That wasn't the last summer I spent with Uncle Ralph. When I was fourteen, the State Department had him assigned to Cairo. We took a trip on camels out across the

Sahara. You have no idea how cold the desert gets at night."

"I—I think I knew that. I r-read a lot."

She reads a lot. He looked down at the way her neck and head dropped forward, and he felt a pinging sensation in the center of his heart. Remembering the romance novel on her coffee table, he also remembered the cover included a European setting. For all her accomplishments and sterling reputation, she had a vulnerability about her that wrenched his heartstrings.

"Tell me more," she said.

He squeezed his eyes shut, steeling himself against the urge to pull her into his arms and promise her the world. He wanted to tell her that her life could change, that it *should* change. She deserved the adventure and excitement that she'd only read about, only dreamed about. Fantasizing visions of them traveling together, he worked his fingers down her spine, making certain not to linger over any one spot. Her slender bones felt feminine, and the skin showing above the silver-dollar-sized button was too inviting. His wandering imagination settled on her here in Florida. He could slide this button through its hole so quickly, allowing the shoulder straps to slip down her arms. His hands could cup her breasts, making beads of the tips as he pressed kisses to that spot above her spine. And then down near the tiny mole. Sinking back on his heels, he drew a deep breath. "Feeling better?" *He* certainly was. He'd been wanting to touch her for days.

"Yes. It's not as stiff."

He cleared his throat. The hell it wasn't as stiff.

"Drew, why are your fingertips rough?"

"Whenever I can, I work on the jobs. I haul rocks. Dig holes for the shrubbery. That kind of thing." He shrugged. "It gets me out of a three-piece suit." His gaze was fixated on the white hair, barely visible in the waning light, between her shoulder blades. What had they called it as children? Angel hair. He lifted his hand to trace her spine again but lowered it after a second thought. She'd accepted his touches in the guise of a therapeutic massage, but to skim his fingertips over her now would be asking for the wrong reaction. "Enough about me. What about you?"

"There's nothing exciting to tell. My mother was ill, and my father . . . wasn't around when I was growing up. I took care of my brother from when he was very young. He's such a good kid. He's in medical school now. Don't get me wrong—there were some rough times along the way. Kids can do dumb things."

"Oh, don't I know it. I was married for a short time during college. Both my father and my uncle tried to tell me she was just like my stepmother," he said.

She raised her shoulders in an enormous sigh, making the nape of her neck look all the more vulnerable. Someday soon he was going to kiss that part of her, that small area where her blond hair touched and the top of her spine began. Right now he had to stop looking at it. Standing up, he brushed the sand from his knees and shins. "Let's walk," he said, offering his hand. As soon as she was on her feet, he let go. Touching her any longer would have been too tantalizing. In that brief moment he held her hand, her silken skin sent a bolt of desire straight to his groin. Shoving his hands in his pockets, he walked through the ankle-deep surf beside her. "You said he's in med school? Sounds as if you did a good job, Jill."

"I think I did." She screwed up her mouth in an attempt at self-effacement. "Does that sound like bragging?"

"Sounds like a proud sister."

"How did you know that's exactly what I wanted to hear?" she asked, reaching for his elbow and giving him a playful shove.

Sidestepping deeper into the surf, he felt her hands close around his elbow, then drag him back up the sandy incline.

"Fine," he said teasingly. "Pay you a compliment, and you throw me to the sharks."

"But I saved you," she teased in return. "I worked as a lifeguard one summer." Reaching behind her back, she laced her fingers together and walked on beside him.

Her soft blond curls blew in the breeze, haloing her head in moving threads of light. No matter that he wanted to guide her to a warm spot beneath the palms; his decision to slow down the inevitable sexual path they were on provided him with something else to cherish. Being with her was like being with a rose opening to the sunlight and accepting that there was no way to rush it. Besides, her spontaneity was a promise of things to come.

"Those Japanese lanterns hanging on my balcony? They were from Peter's high school graduation party. He was valedictorian."

"Does your brother visit you often?"

She shook her head. "He's up in Boston. Traveling takes too much time away from his studies. Besides, it's so expensive. We have to watch . . . that." Looking over her shoulder, she suddenly turned around. "Drew! The tide. It's taking our stuff!"

Together they broke into a dead run. Drew reached the chair first, tossing it up on the sand. "What are you doing?" he asked, as she ran out a few yards into the water.

"Your bag!" she shouted, dragging it out of the surf. Peeking inside, she handed it to him with a skeptical look.

He pulled out a dripping loaf of bread and tossed it to an ecstatic flock of gulls. "That and a hunk of Gouda were going to be my dinner."

"I guess you packed your survival bag for Madrid and not for these harsh Florida winters. Anything else get ruined?" she asked on a more serious note.

He looked in, then made a face. "Well, there went the flaming cherries jubilee. Say, have you had dinner yet?"

"No," she said, not bothering to hide her laughter.

"Uncle Ralph tells me there's a good barbecue restaurant over on Highway Forty-one. Would you like to join me?" He sensed her indecision. "Take pity on poor little Andy. His uncle's threatened to kill him. This might be his last meal. His last chance to play miniature golf. Ah, hell, Jill. I just want to see more of you."

She regarded him openly, and in that moment he felt his heart stand still. Then, in the dimming light, he saw something around her eyes and mouth ease. Something sweet. Something warm. Something irrevocable. His heart pounded at her reply.

"This was inevitable, wasn't it?"

SIX

Her practical decision to date Drew made perfect sense. The more they were together, the less time he had to play private detective.

Walking along Nutmeg Court in the balmy afternoon, she mulled over the last week with Drew. Practical? Sensible? Shaking her head, she almost laughed out loud. This breezy, lighthearted mood was one she wasn't used to. Continuing to rationalize her time with him wasn't necessary anymore. Drew hadn't mentioned burglaries all week, and she had almost forgotten them as well. She'd been too busy enjoying his attention. Whether it was the miniature-golf game or their evening at the dinner theater, she had never had more fun. She laughed more nowadays, a lighter, yet somehow richer, laugh that came up from her toes. There were so many things she was learning about him. And so many more things she'd yet to know. Why he'd chosen his career. What he did for Christmas. When he got the scar on his finger. Why he said good night with one chaste kiss.

That last, unvoiced question had her in more of a turmoil than anything. With every step she took, guilt tinged the pleasure. Jill stopped by a hibiscus bush long enough to twist off a yellow blossom. Until meeting Drew, she'd been able to sidestep her personal problems by centering her life around other people's problems. Sidestepping the personal problem confronting her now was not so easy or desirable. She'd always been proud of her self-control, but Drew was a master of his. He promised he'd prove to her this thing between them was more than a sexual attraction.

"You have!" she wanted to shout. "But what are we going to do about that sexual attraction?" she longed to whisper.

She was doing it. Acting like a carefree teenager doing the one thing she said she wouldn't do. She was filling up that place inside her marked DREW WEBSTER, and falling in love with him in the process. Stopping again, she stared down at the flower. What an insane, untimely, illogical idea, loving Drew. Loving Drew. One week ago she feared him meddling in her affairs. Now she couldn't wait to see him. And this time when she did, she wasn't going to wait for his one chaste kiss. She rounded the last corner. This time she—

She spotted him in the Lockwood's side yard pointing at a trellis, then gesturing toward the carport. Bob Lockwood looked toward a neighbor's yard and nodded. Disappointment struck her like a coconut hitting concrete. Drew hadn't given up. He was out stirring up the neighborhood. Damn him. He hadn't even kept his promise about being the invisible man! How many others had he been talking to?

Cinnamon Key was her responsibility. Why hadn't he told her he was going ahead with his original plan to canvass the neighborhood? Closing her eyes for a second, she reached down deep for the Jill Stuart she used to be, the one who hadn't yet begun to love Drew. What a wasted search. The time before she began to love him wasn't worth reviewing. *This isn't fair, Drew*, she wanted to shout, while emotional anarchy was wreaking havoc with her mind. Disappointment stung with every step as she walked across the street, through Bob Lockwood's petunias and over his lawn. She had to know what was going on.

"What's up?" she asked, a little too brightly.

"We've got problems here, Jill," Bob Lockwood said. "Drew's been filling me in on the bad news."

"He has?" she asked, glaring at Drew. Drew's welcoming smile turned into a puzzled expression. "Drew doesn't live here, Bob," she said, straining for a lighthearted tone. "What would he know about Cinnamon Key that I wouldn't?"

Bob Lockwood removed his cap and scratched his forehead. "What he says makes sense, Jill. We'll all have to be more careful. I think we should call a meeting in the clubhouse."

"There's no cause for panic. If any laws were broken, I'm sure I'd have been told about it, and then I would have alerted the neighborhood. That's the way we do things here. Don't you agree?"

Shoving his hat in his back pocket, Bob gathered up his hose and hung it on the rack. "Don't blame yourself, Jill, but I think you missed this one. And, anyway, it's a community problem, and we're all going to have to act on it." He turned back to Drew. "Well, I'm going in now for my dinner. Drew?" Shaking Drew's hand, Bob nodded thoughtfully. "Can't thank you enough for your input on this."

When Bob was out of earshot, she gave Drew a withering look. "How could you do that? I thought we'd settled that crazy idea of yours about burglaries."

"Calm down," Drew urged, reaching for her arm. He knew he shouldn't be surprised at her jumping to this conclusion, but he was surprised at her genuine flare of anger toward him before hearing his explanation. Moving out of his reach, she walked on down the drive to the sidewalk, carefully avoiding the bank of white petunias. He followed, chuckling to himself. "Wait up, Jill."

She halted, then turned on her heel, shaking the hibiscus at him. "You're laughing! There are people across the street whose respect I treasure, and you're laughing at me in front of them. This is my life you're toying with. Damn you, Drew!" Flinging the flower at him, she walked past him and back toward Cinnamon Circle.

He followed her, waving at the walkers who had stopped to stare first at Jill and then at him. According to the look on half the people he'd passed, he'd become the neighborhood villain. The other half appeared mildly amused, and one man yelled, "Don't let her get away, son."

The gentleman's heart was in the right place, but Drew's impatience with Jill was growing into exasperation. By the time he'd reached her bottom step, he was beyond exasperation. Way beyond. Hadn't all that time together during the last week meant anything to her? Changed anything in her? It had in him. He'd even begun considering moving South and running his company from there. Good Lord, he was on the verge of changing his life to be with her, and she was throwing things at him and damning him in the process. He looked down at the crushed hibiscus flower in his hand and swallowed uncomfortably.

Waiting a respectable thirty seconds, he climbed the steps and raised his hand to the door. This was not the time for polite hesitation. Opening the door, he shoved it hard, letting it bang back against the wall.

She must have heard him coming up the stairs. Her hands were at her hips, and with her eyes leveled at the door, she looked as if she was ready for battle. So was he. "What the hell is going on?"

"You didn't knock," she said, avoiding his question with a raised chin and exaggerated politeness.

"You didn't lock your door."

Her chin went higher. "I told you, I don't lock my door."

"And I told you, with me around, you'd better."

Leveling a finger in his direction, she took a step toward him. "Forget the door. For the last week you led me to think you'd put aside this burglary nonsense. It's the piano, isn't it? You think Barbara's a ditsy old woman. You've been pretending you believed her explanation about the piano. Drew, no burglar in his right mind would steal a piano!"

Reaching behind him, he shoved the door closed. "Don't you think I know that?"

"So what were you doing talking to Bob about burglars?"

"Let's back up a little, and I'll—"

"I don't want to back up. You've as much as lied to me, letting me believe everything was fine, that I could trust you not to—to—"

"To what, Jill?"

"To embarrass me. Drew, you should have told me before you started talking to my—to the residents." In a gesture of pure frustration her fists came up to the sides of her face. "You never should have done that. I thought, especially after this week when we spent so much time with each other, that I could depend on you not to betray me this way."

Looking away from her, he asked in an incredulous whisper, "Is that really what you think of me?" After a quiet moment he looked back at her. "I haven't betrayed you, and I hope you know I'd never embarrass you. Bob Lockwood and I were talking about xeriscaping."

She opened her mouth and closed it twice. "What?"

"Xeriscaping. Water conservation. Drought-resistant plants. Resource management. Your residents use water as if it's liquid sunshine." Her stricken look turned to one of embarrassment and then laughter. Sinking onto the back of the sofa, she drew her fingers down her face.

"Oh, Drew," she finally managed, "I thought you were still playing detective."

"And what if I were? What would be so terrible? Here's the truth, Jill. I've kept my promise to you. Except for you and Uncle Ralph, I haven't talked to anyone about my concerns for security around Cinnamon Key." He held up his hand when she smiled too quickly. "But don't misunderstand me. My ears and my eyes have always been open. Every night I'm out walking around the neighborhood." Her face contorted to a pinched look of panic.

"Why?"

"Why not? I'm concerned about my uncle. Even if he says he has changed his mind about burglaries, he's as preoccupied with Barbara Brody's welfare as he's ever been. When I ask him about it, he tells me there's no cause to worry." He watched her eyebrows go up. "Something's still out of whack here."

"Maybe your uncle is interested in Barbara in a more personal way."

"What's that supposed to mean?"

She shrugged and looked away. "Maybe he wants to date her."

"Date her? Boy, you pulled that one right out of thin air." He shook his head.

"Why is that such a hard thing to picture, Drew?" she asked, insistence building in her voice. "They're old, not dead."

"Because if it were that simple an explanation, he would have told me. We're open books to each other," he shot back. Except that he'd kept his deepening feelings about this blond fireball to himself. He rubbed his head in confusion; this wasn't like him. He detested keeping secrets. Annoyed with himself, he tried picking up where he'd left off. "Look, I wanted to tell you that I'm quietly watching out for anything suspicious." He jabbed a thumb against his chest. "The reason I haven't mentioned it is because I thought you'd react exactly the way you are reacting. As if nothing's wrong. As if nothing's ever been wrong or ever will be wrong. Can't you feel it? Can't you feel there's something a little off-center going on around here?"

"But there isn't anything—"

"Just tell me the truth. If there *was* something wrong, you wouldn't ask for my help. Would you?" Her eyes darted from his stare, losing their focus in a flash of cogent awareness. "I thought so," he said regretfully. Walking back to the door, he looked once over his shoulder. Her expression hadn't changed; his eye-opening words had hit the mark. Quietly setting her lock, he walked out and closed the door. Halfway down the steps he heard her struggling to open her door.

"Wait!" she shouted.

He stopped but didn't turn around.

"I . . ."

He waited an eternity, and when one passed without a word from her, he took another step down the stairs.

"Help . . . me."

Turning around, he walked back up the stairs. There was still a timid look, a hesitation, to her expression. He had no idea what she was going to ask him, but the important thing was that she'd called him back. The walk down the steps had taken the marrow out of his bones, but he gladly would have crawled on his hands and knees over hot coals to get back to her.

"At your service, Miss Stuart. What would you like me to do?" He watched her tuck a curl behind her ear.

She looked up. "I, uh. There's going to be a wedding at the gazebo tomorrow afternoon."

"I know. Nora Plimpton's got Nutmeg Court in an uproar. Go on. You're doing fine."

She smiled at his words of encouragement. "I hate to ask—"

"Because you'd rather give blood to a terrorist than ask for help."

"I need someone to pick up two topiary angels from the Orange Blossom Nursery out by Macomber. They have to be in place at the gazebo at three o'clock, and Orange Blossom won't have them ready until two. I'd get them myself, but—"

"Topiary angels?" he said, then grimaced.

"I know. They sound perfectly horrible, don't they?" Her tension broke, falling away with a roll of her eyes and a whimsical smile. "The bride has this thing about angels, and when she found out that nursery makes them out of lemon leaves, she had to have them. She said this was her third and last wedding, and this time she was going to have angels." Jill stopped for a moment, looking from side to side. "Why are you smiling like that?"

"I was picturing topiary angels." But he wasn't. He was thinking about Jill and the step forward she was taking. A step toward him and the inevitable moment when they were going to make love. Once that happened, once he'd experienced the deepest essence of her, she was never going back to that singular world she hid in. Whatever secrets she kept from him would at last be his. Then he would have what he'd always wanted but never had a name for until now. Jill. All of Jill.

Her eyes had taken on extra sparkle, but her

gaze was darting to and from his own. Whatever she was thinking about had her shimmering with renewed tension. Reaching out to her, he drew his thumb across her cheek, while desire shot through him like a flaming arrow. He forced his thoughts from the throbbing ache in his groin. He needed her, but he needed to get away from her too. Like a rose, she would open to him when the moment was right. Slipping his hand in his pocket, he watched her eyes a little longer. They burned with a myriad of questions he was going to love answering. Her passion was a wild card, and he was certain when she played it, they were both going to win. "Don't worry about the angels. I'll have them here in plenty of time," he said, heading down the steps.

Someone had turned on a tape of *Trumpet Voluntary* while Jill checked and rechecked the list on her clipboard. The caterers were inside the pink lawn tent putting the final touches on the tables, forty gilded chairs were perfectly arranged in curved rows by the gazebo's steps, and the open-air structure itself was aflutter with silk moire ribbons.

Weeks ago when Nora Plimpton had described her dream wedding, Jill had kept her doubts to herself. Now she was glad she had.

What had sounded like a garish reproduction of a Las Vegas wedding chapel was turning out to be a romantic valentine. And she was trapped in the middle of it, complete with music, waiting for two topiary angels, and Drew. Resting her clipboard on the back of a chair, she gave in to fantasy, allowing herself to be swept away by swirling hazy images.

Drew taking her in his arms and dancing her around the gazebo.

She was wearing a white dress and baby's breath in her hair. . . .

They were laughing at the angels . . . and kissing . . . and kissing . . . and—

"Miss? Excuse me?"

"I'm terribly sorry," she said, jerking her fingers from her lips as her clipboard landed at the feet of the caterer's assistant. "My mind was on something else. Is there a problem?"

The young man held out a white swan cleverly molded in hardened sugar. "The boss wanted your approval. He wanted me to assure you that sugar swans hold up better in this heat than white chocolate ones."

She felt herself being sucked into sensory overload, but at the moment she didn't care. "They're adorable. I mean, I'm sure the bride-to-be will be pleased," she said, reaching out to touch a wing.

"You're just the wedding coordinator?" he asked, pulling the swan out of her reach.

Her gaze flicked to the young man's face. "Y-yes. Just the coordinator," she said, stumbling over the simple words as if they were a murder confession. She watched dumbly as the assistant shrugged and headed back to the tent. *Swans. Trumpet music. Angels!* Scooping the clipboard from the lawn, she looked again at the gazebo. *Dancing with Drew. Kissing . . .* Drew hadn't kissed her, hadn't *really* kissed her, in days. Even the day before, when he'd agreed to pick up the angels, when he'd had the perfect opportunity to kiss her, he hadn't. She winced and shook her head. Holding her dreams about Drew in check had never been easy, but as she remained in the middle of this romantic fantasyland, the task was proving impossible.

She gritted her teeth. Nothing was impossible. Hadn't she proved that by surviving those early years? By sending Peter to medical school? By keeping her word to Barbara? By not allowing herself to be an impractical, irresponsible, starry-eyed female? She rubbed her temples as a dull ache began pulsing there. "Somebody turn that music down!" she shouted.

She glanced at her watch. Quarter of three. Why wasn't Drew there? Why had she ever asked him to get those angels? And why had the assistant caterer's innocent remark agitated her? The double squeal of brakes interrupted her thoughts. What now?

Drew and the bride-to-be pulled up to the curb in separate cars and got out. While Drew reached back into his, Nora Plimpton hurried across the lawn to Jill.

"Jill, there's been a snafu. Our best man and matron of honor just called me. Their plane was rerouted to Chattanooga." Cupping her hands over the hot rollers covering her head, she gave Jill a pitiful look. "I have to do my hair and—"

"Angels-R-Us," announced Drew, arriving beside them with the two leafy cherubs in his arms. He winked at Jill, then turned to Nora. "A match made in heaven, or if you will, near Macomber."

"Oh, Andy," Nora said, tucking her fingers into a plump ball against her chest. "They look just like the ones in the magazine." Taking one from Drew, she moved to the steps of the gazebo, happily fussing over its placement.

"Doesn't anyone over fifty know that my name's not Andy?" he asked Jill in a stagy whisper.

His baseball cap was on backward, and his T-shirt was ripped in several places, but it was his high-spirited energy that held her attention. He was brimming over with enthusiasm. Narrowing her eyes with suspicion, she swallowed back her laughter.

"You look more like an Andy than a Drew," she said, touching a mud smear on his shoulder. Lord, she shouldn't have done that, because she wanted to do it again. She did it again. His muscular arms were firm to the touch, strong enough to wrap around her and . . . she really had to stop this.

"What have you been up to?" she asked, hiding her hand behind her clipboard, where she secretly rubbed the mud between her fingers. "Mud-ball fights?" His gaze moved lazily from his arm to her face. Lifting his eyebrows until they touched the adjustable plastic band across his forehead, he kept them there in challenging silence.

"You *were* in a mud-ball fight, weren't you?"

Raising his arm from his side, he glanced down at his mud-splattered clothes, then gave her a mischievous grin. "No. I got talking to the owners and helping them shift around some shrubbery displays. Orange Blossom Nursery is going out of business in May, and . . . well, never mind that now. We can talk about it later. How's this wedding coming along?"

"Fine."

"Not fine," said Nora, returning to Drew's side. "Mitch and I need a best man and maid of honor." Taking the second angel, she looked first at Drew and then at Jill. "Would you two do me one more tiny favor? Would you stand up for me and Mitch?"

Thumping a hand to his chest, Drew staggered back with mock surprise.

"Oh, you don't need a tuxedo," explained Nora. "Just something you can wear with a tie. Please say you will."

Shrugging good-naturedly, he pinched at his T-shirt. "A tie and a shower," he said. "How about it, Jill?"

"Yes, how about it, Jill? I already know what you're planning to wear. You'll look marvelous in that pink lace, dear." Nora winked at Drew. "She has this simply gorgeous pink lace dress, strapless and just to the knees," said Nora, indicating the length of the garment was a generous few inches shy of the knees.

Jill stared back at both of them, surprising herself as she considered the request. Nora didn't have time to start calling people. How bad could it be standing across the steps of the gazebo from Drew while they listened to wedding vows? Her heart sank to her stomach at the next thought. How bad could it be, pretending she wasn't pretending that this was their wedding? Was she crazy to think she could get through that and the reception too?

Before she could decide, Drew decided for them. With two thumbs up to Nora, he accepted before Jill could say no.

"Forty-five minutes," declared Drew, pumping his arms furiously as he ran backward to his car. "You won't recognize me."

She recognized him. He was the handsomest man at the wedding. He wore a navy-blue blazer, a red rose in his lapel, and a serious expression throughout the brief ceremony. His gaze kept drifting her way, perfectly timed to meet her own searching one. She kept looking down at the flowers in her hands, steeling herself against the words of Kahlil Gibran and the crushing weight in her chest. Love. One more word about everlasting love, and she thought she'd explode. By the time she returned Nora's bouquet, her eyes were stinging and her lungs were working far below capacity.

After the ceremony the trumpet music flared to a crescendo, painfully vibrating her tear ducts in the process. She had to get her mind off Drew and onto something else. Plastering an idiotic smile on her face, she looked around. It was an elegant affair; everyone was saying so. Even Max, sporting a black bow tie and sturdy leash, sat quietly in Barbara's lap, at least until someone tossed rose petals into the air. When Drew kissed the bride and congratulated the groom, tears pricked at Jill's eyes, and she knuckled them away before anyone could see. In the spirit of the moment he kissed her, too, and suddenly it was all too precious, too silly, and too wonderful to stand another minute.

Excusing herself, she slipped quietly away to the lawn tent. "Do something," she whispered, looking frantically around her. There must be something that needed taking care of, something she had to do. Something important and necessary. Something to keep her away from Drew. She straightened chairs, fussed over flowers, and began a tug-of-war with the caterer over the cake plates.

"Troublemaker."

She didn't have to turn; she didn't have to look. The sound of his teasing voice, the prickles down her spine, and the way she forgot to breathe told her it was Drew. "I just wanted to help," she explained lamely. When she heard him coming closer, she arched away, reaching for a tray of champagne. The caterer slid it away. If Drew touched her, there would be no turning back. "I'm sure I'm needed here."

"You're not. You're needed out there," he said, taking her hand to lead her out of the tent. When she resisted, he leaned close to her ear. "I need you out there," he whispered.

For the next hour he never left her side. She tried slipping away once, but his reach was discreet, his grasp firm, and his attitude determined. He brought her back to his side, bumping her hip twice for good measure. And because it felt good. Too good. After that, he made certain his hand lingered at the small of her back. During the afternoon she stopped looking for an escape, but he was never sure when that was. His attention revolved around her gestures, each guileless and feminine and leaving him momentarily speechless. The way she touched her earring while she tried to recall something. When she steadied herself on his arm to adjust her shoe. Peeking at him over the rim of the glass when she thought he wasn't looking and wouldn't know. He knew. Every physical detail was indelibly printed in his consciousness. After a time he stopped the social charade, directing all of his attention on her. The hour moved on, slowly and hypnotically as a summer fog.

He blinked; she was saying something about the cake.

"Lilacs made of white icing. That's the prettiest cake I've ever seen, Nora."

She reached for a plate, but Drew took it first. "One's enough," he explained, pulling her across the lawn and up the steps into the empty gazebo.

"We're not going to dance, are we?" she asked, a hint of panic evident in her quick question. "I mean, I don't mambo very well."

"You're in luck," he said, feeding her a forkful of cake. "Neither do I." He ate a bite, then put the plate on the wide white rail. When he looked up at her again, the party was happening somewhere far away. Even the silk ribbons hanging from the rafters seemed to be twirling in another universe.

With a delicate stroke of her fingertip, she wiped icing from her mouth, then pointed at his. And then, miraculously, she reached for his mouth. "You have some . . ." She wasn't talking anymore; she was staring at him with a new kind of intensity. The world jolted to a stop, and for a moment the only thing existing was the warmth of her fingertip. Taking her hand, he dragged her finger across his lips, then licked it. She moved closer inside the space that was theirs now, her blue-green eyes widening with awareness. "Jill?" Gathering her into his arms, he kissed her and kept on kissing her until his throat hurt.

"They won't miss us," she whispered against his face.

He waited until he could safely move. "Go on ahead. I'll be right behind you."

Five minutes later he opened her door, then walked inside with a bottle of champagne. Giving the door a gentle kick to close it, he leaned back against it. "Hi."

"Hi." Moistening her lips, she hesitated. "Here we are," she said, shrugging.

A shock of his hair had fallen forward on one of his eyebrows. "Yes. Here we are," he said, pushing it back.

She wiped her palms together, then tried to run her fingers casually through her hair. Knocking off one of her earrings, she caught it, then hurriedly tried reclipping the gold-jacketed pearl to her ear. "Look at me, I'm a mess," she said, laughing nervously. He came to her, taking her hand and leading her into her bedroom, where he plunked the champagne onto her dresser. Staring into the mirror, he waited until her eyes met his in the mirror, then spoke to her reflection.

"Before we end up discussing who's more nervous, I want to make my intentions perfectly clear." Reaching into his pocket, he took out a foil-wrapped square and placed it next to the magnum. When she didn't move, he took out two more, stacking them on the first. Several seconds ticked by.

Picking up the prophylactics, she turned from the mirror and walked to her bedside table. Slipping out of her shoes, she kicked them aside, smiling at him. "I wanted to make my intentions perfectly clear, too, but I don't have any of these."

The air surrounding them hummed with electricity. "That's okay," he said, stripping off his tie while he moved toward her. Taking the packets, he placed them on the bedside table and smiled at her. "We can share mine."

They were out of their clothes and tumbling back against the pillows in a flurry of moves that left them laughing breathlessly. He rolled to his side and, with his face over hers, stared down into her blue-green eyes. "It had to be on these sheets, didn't it?"

These sheets. The ones he'd helped her fold. The ones she'd watched him hold and touch and rub until she couldn't look anymore. "Yes," she said, winding her fingers through his hair and looking away. "They've been in the linen closet since that day in the laundry room when you . . . touched them."

He kissed her on the nose. "Truth," he said.

"I put them on two weeks ago. I keep washing them and remaking the bed," she said, hiding her face in her hands and fighting back a gentle laugh.

She was like champagne, a mixture of sparkle and subtlety, and suddenly he was very thirsty. Pulling her hand away, he drew his fingers over her lips, then down over her chest until he was cupping her breast. "I've pictured you on these sheets with your hair all fluffy against the pillow and your arms opened to me. Is that what you pictured?"

"Sort of."

"Sort of," he repeated. She tried hiding her face in the pillow, but he urged her back with a kiss. "Sort of this?" Lowering his head, he pressed lush wet kisses to her mouth, then trailed them down her neck and between the soft mounds of her breasts. She smelled like roses and raspberries and warm, womanly flesh. "Or sort of this?" He felt her breathing quicken as he nibbled her, and then she wasn't laughing anymore.

"Oh, Drew," she whispered, sinking her fingers into his hair. Holding him lightly to her breast, she urged him on with restless movement. Dragging a thumb over her beaded flesh, he rolled it between his fingers, tugging on it softly. He felt her pushing, then pulling, on his arms, mewling his name over and over. He took her other nipple between his lips as he lowered his hand to the soft nest of curls between her thighs. She was hot and moist, opening for him with a breaking moan.

When she cried out his name in tiny gasps, his erection became almost unbearable. If she couldn't last, he was damn well sure he couldn't. He withdrew his fingers, and she twisted into his embrace.

"Baby," he whispered between her kisses, "we can keep this going, but you'll have to help me out. You can't—aahhhhh." Her fingers were closing around him, and she was nudging him onto his back. Grabbing two fistfuls of sheet, he held his breath until she sucked it out of his mouth with a kiss.

"Next time," she said, staring into his half-closed eyes. "Drew, help me. I want us together now."

"Right," he said, reaching for the first foil packet. "Next time . . . we'll go slow." *If he lived through this.* He readied himself with surprising speed and a minimum of fumbling, then turned to take her in his arms again. "Now?"

"Now," she whispered, guiding him to enter her in one smooth and splendid surge. With each stroke his tenderness took her breath away, and his passion brought it back. As his solid flesh filled her, pleasure coiled tighter and tighter. More pleasure than she'd ever known. Pleasure to the limits of her experience and then beyond. Pleasure so intense, her balled fists slipped over his shoulders, then fell open on her pillow. She looked up into his eyes, eyes naked with desire and with determination to please. He was giving so much. "N-now," she whispered, giving it back to him on a breathless cry.

Now and forever, he vowed silently as he

watched her eyes close with that little death. Her spasms brought him to his limit, and he finally gave the rest of himself to her with her second climax.

When it was over, they both lay gasping in each other's arms.

He was the first to speak. "Are you okay?"

"Better than okay."

"Yes, you are," he agreed, easing out of her. "I'll be right back."

When he returned from the bathroom, she was standing at the dresser wrapped in her sheet and opening the champagne.

"Be careful where you point that thing," he said, before the cork ricocheted off the wall and across the room. Champagne foamed out of the bottle and down the sheet that was draping the front of her.

Shaking his head in mock dismay, he crossed the room, holding his hand out for the bottle. "An '83 Taittinger. Do you know how much this stuff costs?"

She nibbled the inside of her cheek as she handed over the still-gurgling bottle. "Plenty," she said, when she was sure she wouldn't laugh. She watched as he placed it on her dresser. "How did you get this past that grumpy caterer?"

He peeled the soaked material from her breasts and belly, then knelt at her feet. "He gave it to me," he said, licking her belly. As his hands came up to cup her buttocks, he felt her shudder in surprise. His tongue went lower. She twisted the corner of the sheet and moaned. "Jill?"

She moaned again, and he whispered, "Slowly this time?"

"I'll try," she said, letting go of the sheet and tangling her fingers in his hair, "next time."

SEVEN

He'd waited so long to wake up with his hips pressed against her bottom. So very long to know her this way. Running his hand over the curve of her waist, he breathed in her scent and snuggled hard against her. "You smell good," he whispered, kissing that part of her where her hair brushed her neck.

"Drew?"

"Mmmm."

"Drew, you know what happened last time you did that. And we used all three of your . . . 'perfectly clear intentions.'"

Easing back, he rolled her over to face him. "Now's a fine time to turn practical on me," he said, touching her sleep-soft lips. "We're out of my 'perfectly clear intentions' because you insisted showering together would not be a carnal adventure."

"You proved me wrong," she said, stretching lazily in his loose embrace. Her breasts bumped his chest, and she held them there while her eyes widened with heat. "And you proved it so well," she whispered.

He swallowed with difficulty, then lifted himself away from her and up into a sitting position. "I think we'd better talk about something else. At least until I get to a pharmacy."

"Yes, I think so too." Scooting up, she arranged the sheet to cover her breasts. "This peach pattern doesn't match the fitted," she said, referring to the sheet she pulled out of the linen closet last night to replace the one she'd soaked with champagne. The one he'd peeled away from her breasts and belly. She looked over at him, feeling that pull starting again.

Staring straight ahead, he was crossing his arms over his chest and fighting back a grin. "I don't think we ought to be talking about bed linens either. Not with our wet and wild history with them."

"Oh."

His gaze drifted sideways, meeting hers across the few feet separating them. She began to laugh, and he joined her.

Ruffling the hair on the side of her head, she squinched up her mouth. "Let's see. We can talk about the wedding. How did you like Max's bow tie? I can't figure out how Barbara attached it to his flea collar."

Snapping his fingers, he said, "Darn. I forgot. Barbara was looking for you right after the ceremony. It slipped my mind because she left when I found you in the tent." Jill was staring straight ahead, frozen motionless with her own thoughts. "Jill?"

"Did Barbara say what she wanted?"

"No. I'm sure she'll call if she needs you," he said, turning on his side to support himself on one elbow. He smoothed the sheets between them. "Jill, I wanted to talk to you about that nursery over in Macomber. Remember, I told you—"

"What? Oh, hold that thought," she said, slipping out of bed. "I'll make some coffee."

Morning light was sifting through the blinds, making exotic designs of light and shadow on her skin. The sight of her was one more new pleasure to experience. Watching her move naked across the room made him forget whatever he'd been talking about. He decided to settle back and enjoy the scene when she disappeared into her closet. "Do-o-on't!" he wailed, turning the command into a comical cry.

"Don't what?" she asked, twisting around to stick the top half of her body out the door.

"Don't . . . cover your breasts. Don't move. Don't leave me here like this," he said, groaning dramatically. "A man can die in this condition."

"Not if he has his coffee." Slipping into a blue silk robe, she headed for the door. "I'll be right back."

She hurried from the room, leaving him collapsing on his face as she shut the door. One thought pulsed through her mind as she raced to the wall phone in the kitchen. Barbara was looking for her. Worse than that! Barbara, who knew a bookie named Hector, was looking for her. Grabbing the receiver, she punched in the numbers. While she waited, she began imagining all sorts of imminent disasters. They were all her fault too. If she hadn't chosen to spend so much time and thought and energy on Drew, she would have kept better tabs on Barbara. She hadn't had a good talk with her in days.

Shoving her fingers through her unkempt curls, she began pacing in front of the phone. She'd always been there for Barbara, for any of her residents. Now her world was being turned upside down, inside out, because of Drew. She stopped pacing and leaned her forehead against the wall. Drew. Magnificent, funny, intense, wonderful Drew. Her heart ached with the abundance of love she felt for him. How had her life become so complicated? *And why wasn't Barbara answering her phone?*

"Jill?"

In one guilt-driven move she slammed the phone onto its cradle and whirled around to face him. "Drew." She pressed a hand to her stomach as she stared at him leaning against the doorjamb. "You startled me. H-how long have you been standing there?"

Barefoot and shirtless, he pushed off the jamb, his trousers hanging beltless on his hips. "Long enough to know you wish I weren't. What's up, Jill?"

She felt her face coloring and her mouth going dry. "Nothing's up. I was calling . . . my brother, that's all."

Leveling a stare, he said evenly, "I thought we knocked those walls down last night. Come on, out with it." His voice warmed, and the sight of his smile sent a ripple of pleasure through her body as he continued, "Let me help you. You might as well spill it. You know what a determined man I can be."

She would have felt better if he'd been angry. She could handle anger. This confident teasing was another thing altogether. Wrapping her robe tie around her finger, she looked away from him. "Things are happening between us so fast."

"Things were meant to happen between us. The fast part was your fault." When she gave him a weak smile followed by a hopeless look, he smacked the doorjamb hard. "God, Jill, why won't you let me in?"

Panic shimmied through her. "Please, Drew. Why do you want to get involved when your life is in New Jersey? Leave it alone. This isn't your problem."

"Then there is something. Are you in trouble?"

She shook her head a little too hard, then strove to speak carefully. "I told you, if there's trouble around Cinnamon Key, I can take care of it." He waited a long time to speak, and when he did, she felt her new and shining world begin to disintegrate.

He rubbed the back of his neck. "Just tell me something. I need to know about last night."

She scraped her teeth against her lip. "What about last night?"

"Any regrets?"

"None. I'll never regret last night." She stared into his eyes until hers began tearing. She had to change the subject or she'd dissolve into a puddle of tears. Moving toward the table, she closed both hands around the bleached-pine chair. "You wanted to talk about something before. What was it?"

He made a move toward her, then stopped himself. "I better get out of here," he said, dragging his hand over his mouth.

"You can tell me later," she said hurriedly. "We'll have dinner here."

He stared at her for a long time. "Looks as if I'm pushing against brick walls. Maybe I'd better stop for a while." Another painful silence filled the air around him. "Should I?"

She looked up helplessly. "Last night . . . was . . . wonderful."

"Tell me something I don't know."

Her lips parted, but instead of speaking, she lowered her head and blew out softly.

Taking the chair opposite her, he straddled it and sat down. Covering her hand with his, he waited until she looked at him. "I'm flying up to New Jersey this afternoon."

She didn't move, didn't breathe, as she took in the meaning of his words.

"I see." She sat down at the small table, feeling a million dead stars draining from her face. Swallowing the lump in her throat, she held herself rigid in the chair, waiting for the hurt to go away and the anger to begin.

"I'm coming back, Jill. We're going to work this out."

"You don't have to say that," she said, slapping away a betraying tear.

❖───────❖

He wasn't coming back. Not to her, anyway. Not with the way things were.

While she waited for Barbara to answer her doorbell, the thought played over and over in her mind. Drew was never coming back unless she explained the "burglary" myth to him. Today. Before he left. And she couldn't tell him anything until Barbara released her from her promise of silence.

All Barbara had to do was listen to her plan. First she'd swear Drew to secrecy, and then she would tell him everything. Or at least the parts Barbara agreed to.

"Jill, dear," the older woman said, opening the door to her. "Come right in."

To the joyful yapping of Max, Jill went inside and closed the door. "We need to talk, Barbara."

Barbara picked up Max, then quieted him as she sank onto the sofa. "Oh, dear," she said, stroking the little dog's head and making it bob. "You're probably wondering why I wanted to talk to you at the reception yesterday. Well—Jill, you look positively stricken. What's the matter?"

The matter was, for the last hour and a half she'd been so absorbed with Drew's departure, she'd forgotten Barbara had been looking for her. Forgotten that that was the reason she'd rushed out of bed and been caught by Drew while she was phoning Barbara. "Why did you want to see me, Barbara? What's wrong?"

The woman looked nervously from side to side. She stroked Max until the little white dog whined to get down.

"It was a silly thing, really. My car's been acting up, and I wanted to ask if you thought the service station across the causeway was fair. You know how some places take advantage of a single woman."

Jill studied her closely. "Are you sure that's all you wanted to see me about? That bookie hasn't been bothering you, has he?"

"No, Hector hasn't phoned in . . . a long time." She rushed on quickly. "And, as for my car, I asked Ralph where he thought I ought to take it. He says Whelk's Service Station is honest."

Barbara's smile was a bit too wide, her eyes a tad too bright, but for the time being Jill was going to accept what she'd heard. Sighing quietly, she moved to the edge of her chair. "Barbara, Drew and I have been seeing a lot of each other."

"I know, dear. Ralph told me," she said, smiling benevolently. "We've been spending quite a bit of time together too."

"Barbara, we're two adult women." Barbara nodded. "And we can speak frankly." The older woman was still nodding, but her smile was fading. "Drew's concerned about his uncle. If I had your permission to speak to Drew, I'm certain he would understand, and—"

"Jill, I don't want to sound rude, but what business is it of Drew's who his uncle is seeing?" Barbara stood up. "Or where he spent last night?"

"Last night?" Pressing a palm to her breast, Jill stood up beside her. "You two were together last night?"

"Is it that shocking?"

"Barbara, no," she said gently, "it's not shocking. I just didn't realize you two had grown so close."

"We have," she said. "And he's the most romantic, thoughtful man. I never imagined I'd get a second chance at this kind of happiness."

I never imagined I'd have a first chance. "Barbara, have you told Ralph about your finances?"

The older woman's laugh had a distinctly self-deprecating edge to it. "We talked a lot last night. He said he admired me for handling my affairs so well since Raymond died." She stroked her collarbone and looked away for a few seconds. When she spoke again, her voice was dreamy. "Everything was so beautiful. I didn't want to spoil anything. How could I tell him, after he said a thing like that?"

Jill rubbed her palms together, then opened them to Barbara. "Things would be so much easier if I could tell Drew."

"No. You can't tell him," she said, her eyes filling with tears. "Drew and Ralph share so much. Drew's bound to tell his uncle." Barbara sank into a chair and began to cry in earnest.

As she patted Barbara's shoulders, Jill had to agree with her. Drew had told her how much he loved his uncle. And whether out of a sense of loyalty or a desire to protect Ralph from a potentially "money-hungry woman," he probably would share the information with his uncle.

"Are you ever going to tell Ralph you pawned all those things?"

The white head lifted. "Drew thinks you're hiding something from him, doesn't he?"

Jill nodded.

"I haven't been fair to you, making you keep silent," she said, brushing away her tears with both hands. The tears kept coming.

"Barbara, Ralph will understand this money trouble came from Raymond's weakness, not yours."

Sniffing, Barbara pulled a tissue from her sleeve and wiped her nose. A tentative smile appeared across her face. "Maybe I haven't given Ralph enough credit. He's so very understanding."

Jill's heart was drumming against her rib cage with renewed hope. "And now that you two are closer, he'll appreciate your honesty."

"I never thought of it in that way, Jill." Barbara stood up, patting her on the shoulder. "I'm glad we had this talk. You've helped me to see another side of this. Jill, I will tell Ralph. And as soon as I do, you have my permission to tell his nephew."

"You will?" She checked her watch, then looked at Barbara. Drew was probably on his way to the airport. She could catch him, if she left in the next five minutes. "When, Barbara? When do you plan to tell Ralph?"

The older woman's eyes brightened with relief and satisfaction.

"Just as soon as I cash in my CD."

EIGHT

Jill stared hard at what remained of the two-week-old bouquet. Even with her daily pampering of fresh water and nutrient granules, it was impossible to pretend the creamy pink roses hadn't long since passed their prime. In the quiet of her office she picked the enclosed card from the arrangement. Just looking at his handwriting sent a wave of prickles over her skin. She read his message for the hundredth time.

Keep your doors locked—I'm coming back,
Drew

She pulled the vase closer, breathing in deeply, searching for their scent. Nothing. Not a hint of their once-heady fragrance. Cupping a full-blown flower in her hand, she watched helplessly as petals fell into her palm. Staring at them and then at his card, her lips began to tighten. A handful of petals and a one-line message was all he'd left. She shook her head. That wasn't totally true.

He'd left her aching for him.

He'd left her going quietly crazy.

"Fool," she muttered, grabbing the rest of the flowers and pitching them headfirst into the trash, along with his card. He'd left her with an undeniable truth. He wasn't coming back.

Closing her eyes, she clenched her fists and growled. She'd had a life before Drew, and she was going to have one after him too. Sweeping the rest of the petals from her desk, she began straightening her desk pad, then angled her phone precisely on its diagonal. Getting involved with him had been a careless decision from the start. What had she been thinking of, allowing herself to brashly fall in love with a man like Drew Webster, then assume she could let him go without sacrificing a major organ—her heart? She was old enough and wise enough to know better. Repositioning the pencil cup, she began rearranging the pencils.

He could have trusted her.

He could have had a little faith that she knew what she was doing.

He could have been in at least once when she called—

"Can we bother you for a second?"

Both Jill's hands flattened against her chest. "Barbara, how long have you been there?"

Max ran in place beside Barbara, yipping for his freedom. Fixing her gaze on the trash can, Barbara unhooked the leash, allowing Max to make a dash for the sofa and the window behind it.

"Long enough to know you're upset. I hope I didn't have anything to do with this," she said, raising her eyes toward Jill.

"Why would you think a thing like that?"

"Those flowers were from Drew, weren't they? You two are having an argument, I can tell." Barbara made a cursory attempt to smooth her hair. "I'm sorry, Jill, but I never seem to do anything right lately."

Jill was tempted to tell Barbara that the two of them had more in common than Barbara could ever imagine. She narrowed her eyes. Barbara had something on her mind, and it wasn't Drew Webster.

"Drew did send me the flowers, but that was two weeks ago, and now they're simply making a mess all over the place. Anyway, he's back at work where he belongs, and so am I." Indicating her desk with a wave of her hand, she said,

"See? Everything's normal. Now, what can I do for you?"

The older woman hesitated for several seconds before speaking. "I remembered today is the day you go into Macomber if you need office supplies. I was wondering if I could ride along with you. You see, I need to get to Dilby's."

Jill pushed back her chair and stood up, steadying herself on her desk. She was almost dizzy with anticipation. "You mean you cashed in your CD? You need my help to get your things back from Dilby's?"

"No, dear. My car has quit. I need money for a down payment on a new one, and since my silver tea service just sits there on my tea cart tarnishing by the minute . . ."

Red speckles of light were still obscuring Jill's vision. One hint of hope and she was on the verge of passing out. The power of her reaction frightened her, leaving her momentarily speechless. Readjusting the desk pad, she watched an embarrassed Barbara call Max and reattach his leash.

"Forgive me. I was wrong to ask you again. I'll take a taxi."

"No, I'll take you. I was . . . trying to figure out the best time to drive into Macomber." Taking her purse from the bottom drawer, she set it on her desk and reached to push the On button on her answering machine. "Besides, I need a break. Would now be convenient?"

"Yes. Oh, I knew I could depend on you. I'll take Max back home and pack up the tea service," said Barbara, reaching for the doorknob.

Jill rounded her desk, then stopped dead in front of her trash can. The sight of the flowerless stems and leaves was both pathetic and obscene. She swallowed dryly. "Barbara, I'll pick you up in a few minutes. I forgot something."

Jill waited until she had left, then stooped down next to the trash can. Ignoring the thorns, she picked through the stems. When she found Drew's card, it was like finding a part of him, and she hugged it to her. With a painful laugh she held it out. As she ran her fingertip along its edges and over the words, a rush of tender memories filled her heart. Whatever would or wouldn't happen, she knew one thing. One wild and wonderful truth. She didn't want to forget him or what they had shared.

"No regrets, Drew," she whispered. "Never."

The midnight sky over Cinnamon Key was threatening to break apart with rolling thunder. In the intermittent quiet Jill sensed she wasn't alone. She pulled her hands from the pockets of her midcalf skirt and stopped to look behind her. No one was there. Shaking her head, she reminded herself that this was Cinnamon Key, and that she'd been taking this walk nightly for the last three weeks. Determined not to let her uneasiness overtake her, she quickened her pace only after the rain started.

Leaving the sidewalk, she hurried across the grass. Surely, if there was someone out walking, the person wouldn't follow her to the gazebo. Racing to the top of the steps, she turned and stood looking back at the street. Someone was out there standing by a grouping of palms. Damn. She wanted to be alone to figure a way out of this mess with Drew. Sitting down slowly, she parted her knees and dumped the folds of her skirt in its V. Maybe if she sat perfectly still, the dim light from the street lamp wouldn't reach her, and whoever it was would go on.

There. She sucked in her breath through clenched teeth. The person moved again, and for one panic-filled second she wondered if there could be a burglar in Cinnamon Key. She dismissed the ridiculous thought, but her pulse raced anyway as she turned her head to the side. But who was it out there? Squinting into the rain, she pulled in a long, unsteady breath when the draped apparition began moving over the grass.

No, it couldn't be. She rubbed her eyes. The darkness was playing tricks. Or was it all in her mind? She leaned forward, not daring to breathe. "Drew?" she whispered. "Is it you?"

His light beige raincoat billowed in the wind, then slapped around him as he came toward her. Her heart was pounding in her ears, but not enough to obscure his words.

"I told you I'd be back."

She started to speak, then swallowed when nothing came out. He kept on coming in the darkness, until he stood at the bottom of the steps under the overhang. In the faint light of a street lamp, she could see the rain beading on his hair and dripping off his face.

Before she could form a sentence, he was halfway up the stairs, and she was falling into his arms. He felt so good, so solid, so right, pressing against her, rocking her. All fears of losing him vanished, and through their skirmish of kisses and her squeals of delight, she heard him say, "I couldn't wait another day to get back to you."

"I'm afraid to blink. Afraid you'll disappear," she said.

"I'm not going anywhere." Stepping backward down the steps, he waited until she sat down, then knelt eye level with her. "Let me look at you." Closing his hands over her knees, he ran them along her slightly parted thighs. "And let me touch you. Lord, I missed touching you, Jill."

She couldn't stop trembling. Her desire for him was instant and throbbing, and in the emotion-filled silence she knew it was the same for him. "Drew," she whispered. "I can't believe you're here."

Pressing his thumbs on the inside of her thighs, he leaned in to kiss her. The kiss went on forever, sumptuously slow and thorough. "Do you believe it now?"

Running her fingers through his hair and down his neck, she nodded, laughing. "Yes. But how did you know I'd be here?"

"You come here all the time, don't you?"

He sounded so certain. Certain in the way lovers are certain, and the revelation sent her senses reeling. She looked him in the eyes, knowing she had nothing to lose and everything to gain by admitting it. "Every night . . . since you left."

He leaned in, caressing her lips with his mouth and tongue. "Because?"

She sighed. "Because when I'm here, I think about you."

Running her fingers down his chest, she tucked them into his belt. She didn't want to talk—she wanted to feel his mouth on hers.

He bit gently on her bottom lip. "About me . . . and you?" he whispered, as thunder shook them both.

"Yes," she said, opening her legs to pull him closer still.

"Tell me more. Tell me all of it."

"About . . . how it would be to make love to you here."

"Here?" He looked around them. "Right here on the steps?"

She moved her hand lower, curving it over him as lightning crackled in the sky behind him. Loving Drew made her brave, but wanting him so much made her crazy. "Yes, here," she whispered. "Make love to me here." When he shook his head, she knew a moment of pure panic.

Then he smiled, and it was as if he'd never left.

"You don't know how much I wanted to hear you say that," he said, shrugging off his raincoat and dropping it beside her. His gaze never broke from hers as he slid his hands under her skirt. "How much I've wanted you . . . just like this." In the gazebo's sultry atmosphere he began to kiss her thighs, stringing one kiss after another along their tops.

He found the thin material between her legs, and suddenly she was soaked in sensation, and churning and straining for more. "Drew," she whimpered, sinking her fingers into his hair. "I've thought about this every night," she said, barely taking notice that the street lamps had gone dark.

Her whole being pulsated against the insistent strokes of his fingers. Time and place suddenly had no meaning. Pulling him closer, she felt the heat of his mouth on her breast. He sucked on the gauzy cotton until it was wet and the flesh beneath it peaked.

His breath was ragged and vital with need.

As desire engulfed her, she yielded willingly to his unspoken plea. She unbuttoned her blouse, then unfastened the front closure of her bra and peeled away the tulip-shaped satin cupping her breasts. He found her nipple with his mouth and began sucking the stiffened tip while he continued stroking her, sending tingling streams of pleasure in the moist, hot place between her thighs. She'd never known such erotic desperation. When he tugged the material aside and slipped his finger inside, she knew her patience had run out. "Take them off me."

He exhaled a string of curses, and she knew by his fervor that it was from wanting her so badly. She understood completely. Planting her hands on the floor, she tilted her hips, allowing him to impatiently strip them off.

Delving into his pocket, he brought out the small foil packet, then reached for his zipper. "Let me." Reaching for the packet with trembling fingers, she completed the job, then looked up at him. "This is the craziest thing I've ever done."

"It's not done yet," he said. "It gets a little crazier. Remember?"

Parting her thighs, she guided him in, gasping when he filled her. She did remember. His hardness and heat, the swift strokes followed by slow, determined ones, and all the while the pleasure building, intensifying. And there were new things too. His male scent mixing with the rain, the erotic feel of her skirt hiked up to her belly and her bare legs wrapped around his trousers. And out on the edge of her consciousness, a tiny but delicious fear of being discovered.

He was cursing again, and if they weren't so near the final throes of ecstasy, she knew she would have laughed. But she couldn't now, because the power uniting them overtook them in a frenzy, sending them soaring to a place where all emotions met in a fusing force of white-hot fire. When it was over, he held her in reverent silence, and she, in breathless wonder, let him.

He moved first, reaching for his handkerchief, then turning away to right himself. After a moment he sat up, watching her refasten her bra. "That was one hell of a greeting." She started on the buttons of her blouse, not daring to look at him. "Jill?" When she didn't say anything, he lifted her chin. "Why so quiet? Did I hurt you?"

"No. It's just . . . we were crazy. I'm not used to . . ."

"Taking the risk of asking for what you want? Exploding in a man's arms like a wanton? Making me so happy?" he asked, pulling her into his embrace.

"Something like that," she said, pressing her face against his chest and laughing. By the silent rumbles in his chest, she knew he was laughing too. She breathed deeply, shifting more comfortably in his arms. He was there. What was there to fear?

"How long are you staying this time?" she asked. She winced, instantly regretting the slip. She didn't want to know or think about his leaving, yet she couldn't stop herself from twisting to look up at him for an answer. The rain had ended, and the moon was slipping in and out of the clouds, illuminating his serious expression. Maybe she didn't want to know, but she *had* to know. "How long do we have?"

He stared back intently, as if he wanted to say something but couldn't quite make himself. Their recent intimacy was quickly evaporating into a forced and uncomfortable situation. Smoothing her skirt over her legs, she tried for a matter-of-fact tone when she found her voice. "Please forget I asked."

"Why? Isn't the answer important to you?"

"Is it to you?" she asked quietly. When he didn't answer immediately, she felt an ache welling inside her. "I called you four times," she blurted out. "And you were never in."

"I was busy. I had a lot of meetings. But I'm back, and that's what's important." He reached out for her hand, but she pulled it away.

"So busy you couldn't call me once?" she asked in disbelief. She looked at the place on the floor where they'd just made love. Dear Lord, what had she done? "Did you think you could slip me into your busy schedule while you're down here checking on your uncle and then fly back to your real life in New Jersey?" She tried moving farther away, but he took her by the shoulders, pulling her up on her knees to face him.

"Jill, please. If you think I'm taking this, taking us, lightly, you're wrong." He shook her once, hard enough to make her stop struggling. When she did, he relaxed his grip but kept her at arm's length. "Listen to me."

She didn't want to listen to him, but she had no choice. Staring at his chin, she fought to keep her face expressionless. Curiosity got the better of her, and he began to speak only when her gaze drifted up to meet his.

"Remember the morning I left? I found you in the kitchen trying to call someone. When I asked you what was going on, you said, 'Why do you insist on getting involved when your life is in New Jersey?'"

"I don't remember," she lied.

He smiled, then spoke with an intriguing gentleness. "It doesn't matter. I remembered. I got the message, Jill."

She felt her eyebrows kinking. "What message?"

"Even after that incredible night we'd spent together, you still weren't certain you could trust me. Or depend on me." He ran his hands down her arms. "You gave up depending on people a long time ago. It's true. Don't try to deny it."

She nodded, remembering the tough times when she'd gone it alone. When it really mattered, no one cared enough to get involved. Not the few distant relatives who were satisfied to remain distant when her father left, not those snobby bankers who wouldn't listen to anything but their calculators when her brother needed tuition money, not the unfair and impatient landlords she'd had to deal with for those tiny, rundown apartments when her mother was sick. And then there were those few men who, in the end, weren't real men but little boys. She blinked back the tears she'd thought had long since disappeared. Damm it. She hadn't cried in such a long time.

"You got this far in your life depending on you, not on anyone else."

"That's right," she said defiantly. "I had to."

"Jill," he whispered, "now there's someone around you can depend on. Me."

She was shaking her head, trying to dismiss the tickle of hope in her heart. "I can't do this, Drew. I can't live on stolen hours two or three times a year with you."

"I can't either."

"I—I. What did you say?" she asked, stilling her head.

"For the last three weeks I've been preparing to move down here and open another business. Jill, I bought the Orange Blossom Nursery."

Her heart twisted with pleasure and pain, as fresh tears slid down her face. The tension within suddenly broke, spilling out of her with a groaning laugh. "Is this true?" She thumped him playfully on his shoulder. "But why didn't you tell me? Why didn't you call me?"

"Because I swore to myself that the next time I talked to you, everything would be settled, or at least set in motion," he said, shaking his finger at her. "I wanted you convinced beyond a doubt that I do care about you. That I'm here now. That you can depend on me."

His last words sent a sizzle of warning through her. *Depend on him?* She'd never depended on anyone in her life. Even if this was Drew saying it, the idea of depending on someone had her shaking. What if she did depend on him? What if something happened, and he wasn't there for her? Her thoughts were spiraling out of control. What was wrong with her? Wasn't this the crossroad she'd been looking for? When every signal in her heart and soul and mind said yes, why couldn't she take that leap of faith and accept his word?

Lifting her fist from his shoulder, Drew brought it down over his heart. "Baby, you're shaking," he said, cupping his other hand over hers and his own. He crooked his neck to get a better look at her, then said half-apologetically, "I'm not going to rush you into anything. I know this is a shock, and that you'll have to get used to the idea that I mean what I say. And, listen, whatever it is that you won't tell me about, well, I can wait until you're ready. You see, I already trust you." He made a funny face. "Besides, how bad can it be?"

"Drew," she said, shaking her head, "it's not bad. It's just . . . complicated. I gave my word to someone."

"I understand. That's what makes you so special to me. You have more integrity in your little finger than most people have in their entire bodies. I've never known a woman with your sense of loyalty. So if you say it's not bad, then it's not bad," he said, between tiny kisses. "I just can't help wanting to watch out for you and protect you."

"No one's done that for me for as long as I can remember." She felt his hands, firm and sure, tightening around hers. "I think I could like this," she said, more to herself than to him.

"Keep thinking that, and soon you'll accept that what I'm saying is real. Now, let's get you home." He gathered up their things, and together they walked down the steps into the star-filled night.

"Drew? Your uncle's on a fishing trip and won't be back until tomorrow."

"I know."

Her mood was suddenly playful; she didn't bother hiding her smile. "Maybe you'd like to show me how to lock my door from the inside."

He stopped walking. "Is that an invitation to make love to you all night long?"

"Yes . . ."

"Good, because I was planning to do that anyway," he said, following it with a sound kiss.

She tugged him forward over the wet grass toward the sidewalk. The air was fresh, the crickets were tuning up, and the street lamps were back on, lighting the way.

"If we're still alive by morning, I want to take you to breakfast."

"Tomorrow's my day off—"

"I know."

"You remembered that?"

Slipping his arm around her waist, he said softly, "I remember everything about you."

For a second the world stopped spinning, and all that he'd promised seemed close to realization.

He shook his head. "Breakfast isn't enough. I want the whole day with you. And by all means wear that skirt," he added, pretending his request wasn't an intimate one. "You should always wear skirts."

"Any other fashion tips?" she asked.

"I'll let you know."

"Please do."

He cleared his throat. "We're going to rent a boat over near Breezy Palms and take it out on the river."

"Breezy Palms? I'd love to see the place. You know, Merriweather Development owns that."

"I know," he said, smiling mysteriously to himself.

Waking in the morning with her nestled against him, Drew almost canceled plans for their trip to Breezy Palms. He could have spent the day in bed but settled for half the morning instead.

"We'll stop at a deli and have them pack a picnic basket for us," he said, looking across the interior of his rental car as they drove over the causeway. She was staring into the visor mirror, applying gloss with the pad of her index finger. Her lips were slightly parted, and the feminine act had him aroused in a speedy three seconds. He squirmed in his bucket seat for a more comfortable position. There had to be a subject he could talk about without rekindling his need to have her. Clearing his throat, he retrained his eyes to the road. And he'd have to find one quickly, or they'd end up in the water.

"What do you hear from your brother?"

"Peter called last week." Recapping the tube of gloss, Jill dropped it into her purse and turned to him. She raised her eyebrows. "He reminded me his tuition went up."

"Medical school is pretty expensive, I take it. How do you manage?"

"I don't know, but somehow I always seem to come up with the money."

"Look, if you need any money—"

"What? Oh, no. I didn't mean to imply I was looking for money."

"Business is booming. I have more than enough."

She waved her hands. "Absolutely not. I appreciate the offer, but this is something I have to take care of."

It would have stroked his male ego if she had accepted his offer. Looking over at her, he realized she was simply determined to remain independent on this. Whether it was pride or stubbornness, the reason didn't matter. The root of her action was love. He understood that now. Tears pricked at the back of his eyes. He never thought he'd find a woman like Jill, but now that he had, for richer or poorer, he wasn't letting her go. Several minutes passed before he spoke. "If you change your mind, let me know."

For a moment her stare remained unfocused on the dashboard. "What? Oh, I won't change my mind," she said, dismissing the offer with a wave of her hand. "By the way, I know a shortcut to Breezy Palms. If you take this road through Macomber, you can make the turn onto the county road by Dilby's Pawnshop. That cuts out about five minutes, and it will bring us onto the river road."

"Dilby's Pawnshop? I haven't been to a pawnshop since college."

"Really? Well, let me tell you, Dilby's is a treat. They have more . . . stuff in there . . ." Her voice trailed off. "I mean, it looks as if it's bulging at the seams when I've driven by." Suddenly quiet, she planted her elbow at the base of her window and ran her thumbnail along her chin.

So, she'd been to the pawnshop and was trying to hide the fact from him. His imagination sped off on a bizarre trip through some unpleasant situations involving Jill and her finances. Maybe things were tougher for her than he had thought. He stole a glance at her, but she didn't look back. Rubbing his forehead, he sighed in frustration. The hardest part of anything was the waiting. He'd simply have to hang in there until her reluctance turned to acceptance. In the meantime a little nudge wouldn't hurt.

"You look like you have the weight of the world on your shoulders. Want to talk about it?"

"I don't want to bother you. Besides, you must have a lot on your mind with starting up a business and moving down here."

"You know what they say. You divide your problems and multiply your joys when you talk about them." He took her hand from the back of the seat and held it to his lips. "I'm here now, and along with being your lover, I'm your friend. Remember?" He could see from the corner of his eye that she was considering what he'd said. With exaggerated earnestness he continued. "Hey, I didn't botch the gazebo wedding when you let me help, did I?"

He'd caught her off guard, sending her into a fit of laughter. "No, you didn't botch the wedding. Okay, I'll tell you what's on my mind.

Ever since you mentioned Breezy Palms, I've been thinking about Mr. Merriweather, my boss. There'll be a position opening up soon over there. I'm thinking about discussing the position with Mr. Merriweather, if he ever gets around to stopping by Cinnamon Key." She stopped talking, shifting her gaze to her lap when he took the corner near Dilby's Pawnshop.

He drove silently for several minutes, allowing her time to sort out her thoughts and get back to him. Her troubled expression remained until it began to concern him. "You're really distracted over this, aren't you?"

"I can't imagine leaving Cinnamon Key. That community has been my home for more than three years." She shrugged with indecision. "I can't ignore the money. I don't know what to do."

"Letting go is never easy, but you can't take a step forward without leaving at least part of the past behind you. Jill, you can't stay at Cinnamon Key forever."

"I don't know why hearing you say that took my breath away, but it did."

"That's what I'm here for, to take your breath away," he said, pulling the car into the parking lot of the deli. She was smiling again as he removed the keys from the ignition. "Talk to Mr. Merriweather, Jill. Talking never hurts."

Twenty minutes later Drew was rowing their blue-and-red boat from Lazy Days Boat Rentals into a snarly curtain of weeping-willow branches. "We can picnic up there," he said, gesturing with a jut of his chin toward the bank.

"It's like a painting without a frame."

"Better," he said, resting the oars inside the boat. "It's private."

Blissfully private. The curtain of willow branches and several thick bushes screened them from the light boat traffic. Several times during their lunch they heard murmurs of conversation from other boats drifting by. Jill found herself gazing around the romantic space, then back to Drew. He was stretched out on the blanket beside her, watching her every move. Even after their limited time together, she suspected she knew exactly what he was thinking about. His next statement confirmed it.

"We could be making love up here, and no one would know."

She lowered her chin with a skeptical look. "Somehow I think two naked, noisy people would get noticed."

"And here I thought you had an adventurous spirit," he said, shaking his head with pretended disapproval.

"I do have an adventurous spirit," she insisted, leaning down to kiss him. "I'm just not crazy," she said, lifting her mouth with a disappointed sigh. "What you do to me, Drew Webster . . ."

His silent smile was an invitation to a dream. She rubbed her face. "No. Stop this. We have to talk about something else." She looked around her again. "I've never been to France, but I'll bet they have places like this over there."

"France? We could pretend we're in France. We could whisper in French."

The gleam in his eye had nothing to do with pretense. "Drew," she warned, as he sat up and moved closer.

He tickled her behind her ear. "Did I ever tell you how much I love it when you're wearing a skirt?"

"I seem to recall you favoring this one on me last night."

"Yes. This long one, with its yards and yards of soft material," he whispered, lifting the hem above her knee. "Why, a man could get lost in this skirt for an entire afternoon."

"He could? I mean we can't," she protested, even as she took him in her arms. "I don't speak French."

"Here's your first lesson," he whispered against her lips.

NINE

He was whistling as he unlocked his uncle's front door and went inside. "Anybody home?" he asked, noticing the fishing gear, portable radio, and binoculars piled on the floor nearby.

"Drew? I thought you'd get in late last night," his uncle said, backing through the kitchen door and into the foyer. He was holding a fish in one hand and a gutting knife in the other.

"I did."

"Didn't you have that extra key I gave you?"

Drew lifted his hand, jiggling his key ring. "I have it right here. I decided to spend the night at Jill's."

His uncle looked him up and down, then squarely in the eye. Several seconds of nonverbal communication transpired. The old man beamed. "You look happy."

"I am happy," Drew said, shaking his head with the wonder of it. "I'm going to ask her to marry me."

"Outstanding. Congratulations." Ralph waved the gutting knife toward the kitchen. "Come on in here while I finish these, and you can catch me up on what's been happening."

Drew followed him into the kitchen, took two beers out of the refrigerator, and sat down at the kitchen island next to his uncle. "I signed the papers for the Orange Blossom Nursery," he explained, popping the tops on the beer cans. Sliding one toward his uncle, he continued, "Jill doesn't know it, but I've also been negotiating with Merriweather Development for the landscaping contract on Breezy Palms. The people at Orange Blossom told me Merriweather's original choice wasn't coming across with adequate drought-resistant material."

Ralph wiped his hands on a paper towel and reached for the beer. "Here's to the future."

"The future," Drew said before taking a swallow. "Strange how this all began with that bogus burglary business." He turned to his uncle, who was looking at him from the corner of his eye. Drew's certainty began wavering. "Bogus. Right?" When his uncle didn't answer, Drew set the can on the island. "Out with it. What's going on?"

"I was at Barbara's for breakfast a few mornings ago. She's got a potted fern sitting on her tea cart instead of her silver tea service."

"Did you ask her what she did with the silver?"

"She said she lent it to Mary Kozlowski."

Drew felt the muscles in the back of his neck begin to relax. "There. Geez, you had me going for a minute." The old man continued staring unblinkingly at Drew. "Arrrgh!"

Ralph went on, never missing a beat. "Mary Kozlowski has been on a cruise for over two weeks and won't be back until next Thursday. I've seen that silver at Barbara's since Mary left, so I know she didn't lend it to Mary."

For a moment neither said anything. Then Drew spoke in a hesitant tone, carefully choosing his words. "Is there a chance that Barbara Brody is suffering memory loss?"

Picking up his scaler, Ralph dragged a second, larger fish closer and answered firmly, "No. Right now she's with her book-discussion group at the Hemingway house in Key West. And if your next question is, is she wacko? the answer again is no."

Drew stood up and, rubbing the back of his neck, began pacing the kitchen. "Is it possible she's selling off her things because she needs the money?"

"Out of the question, Drew. Dr. Brody was a successful physician. Besides, Barbara has never shown a sign that she's scraping by in her widowhood." Ralph plunked the fish on the newspaper. "It hurts when you care about someone and she doesn't trust you enough to confide in you."

Thinking about Jill, Drew laid his hand on his uncle's shoulder. "I understand," he said, "but these things usually have a way of working themselves out to a satisfying conclusion."

"Thank you for that advice, Mr. Voice of Experience," Ralph said without any enthusiasm.

Drew sighed. "Let me assure you, Uncle, that that is a title I am earning."

Slipping her checkbook into a kitchen drawer, Jill reached for her tennis racket and can of balls. Usually, her stomach was in a knot after one of these sessions, but today all she felt was a tickling sensation. After going over the figures, she was finally satisfied she would be able to cover Peter's tuition. She smiled as an odd picture entered her mind. Untethered threads were weaving themselves into a strong and beautiful ribbon circling around her and Drew. Things were working out.

Drew was right when he'd said that in order to move forward, you had to leave part of the past behind. She was looking forward to leaving the subterfuge behind her. How blessed she was that Drew trusted and respected her enough to be patient with her a little longer. Indulging herself with future possibilities, she tucked the can under her arm, leaned against the wall, and reached for the ringing telephone in a dreamlike state. "Hello?"

"Hello, Jill. This is Barbara Brody. I'm calling from Key West."

Jill came off the wall and to attention in less than a second. Something was wrong. She knew it the instant she heard Barbara's voice.

"Are you okay?" she asked, alert for the worst from Barbara.

"Yes, but the bus broke down, and since there isn't another available, we're all stuck in Key West for another night."

"Well, that's not such a bad place to be stuck," she said, pressing her backside to the wall and sliding down to rest on her haunches. Several seconds elapsed without further word from Barbara. Her stomach was in knots. "Is there something else you want to tell me?"

"I'm afraid there is, Jill. We were due back in plenty of time for me to take care of a little business matter."

"Business matter?" Jill pressed her hand to her forehead.

"Hector called me."

Jill closed her eyes. "Hector the bookie?"

"Yes. He convinced me to pay off the rest of Dr. Brody's bill by tomorrow night. You see, Hector's planning a trip to Buenos Aires and, well . . . anyway, I was going to take a diamond necklace to Mr. Dilby in the morning. Jill, I need your help." Barbara's words began to rush out in breathless desperation. "I swear this is the last time. There's no one else to turn to but you."

Jill shoved her fingers through her hair, giving it a punishing yank. *The last time. Definitely!* Resigned to the inevitable, she tried for a perky voice. After all, what was one more favor with less than a week to go? "Okay, Barbara. Tell me exactly what you want me to do."

"So Jill's off to see a friend in Fort Myers tonight," Ralph said, gathering up his fishing rods in the foyer.

"Worked out well. This way I get to eat the smallest pan-fried grouper I've ever seen, and I get to spend a few hours with you. I hope we leave enough for your dinner with Barbara tomorrow," Drew said, laughing with his uncle as he reached for the binoculars. "Are these the glasses we bought in Switzerland?"

"The same and good as new," Ralph said, heading toward the back of the house with his gear. "I'm going to call Barbara's to see if she's back. Why don't you try them out on the sign up by the gatehouse?"

Drew went out onto the porch. Raising them in the direction of Cinnamon Circle, he held them steady, focusing them. What he saw first delighted, then confused, him.

In the evening dusk he saw Jill looking over her shoulder, then climbing Barbara Brody's steps. "That's odd," he mumbled to himself. She was supposed to be playing night tennis with a friend over in Fort Myers. Steadying the binoculars, he saw she wasn't dressed for tennis. Then he saw her unlock Barbara's door and go in. Several possible explanations came to mind, but none satisfied him. And then an incongruous possibility began taking control of his thoughts. He laughed out loud, trying to dismiss the ugly idea. It refused to go away.

"Uncle? I'm going out for a few minutes," he said, setting down the binoculars inside the door before closing it.

Drew was out on the sidewalk and walking toward Mrs. Brody's without waiting for his uncle's reply. A jumble of emotions was pricking at his mood, but foreboding won out as he stared at the Brody house. Jill hadn't turned on the lights; what was she doing inside in the dark? He waited, half-hidden by a hibiscus, near the end of the walkway.

Jill came out in less than a minute, not bothering to look over her shoulder as she locked the door. Glancing at something in her hand, she slipped the object into her pocket and hurried down the walkway. Drew's heart thudded sharply in his chest. He didn't want to think what he was thinking, but he couldn't stop himself.

"Hello, Jill."

"Drew?" Her hands flew to her mouth and stomach. Several seconds ticked by before she forced a laugh from her lungs. "Honestly, you gave me a scare."

"Did I?" he asked quietly.

"Yes, you did," she said, brushing her fingers through her hair in that way she had when she was nervous. "Don't tell me you're out trying to catch a burglar," she said, trying for a lighthearted laugh and missing the mark again.

He took a step toward her. "Have I caught one?"

She didn't know whether to be angry or scared. Worse, she didn't know how to read him. While the street lamp made harsh shadows on his face, his voice was distractingly neutral. Where were his understanding looks and his patient voice when she needed them? Couldn't he tell she was teetering on the borderline of panic?

Studying her, he chewed the inside of his cheek. His nostrils flared a second before he spoke. "I believe it's time for that explanation you've been promising me."

Her eyes widened at his insistent tone. She certainly hadn't enjoyed tiptoeing through Barbara's in the dark. Neither did she enjoy being treated like a felon by the man she loved. Lowering her chin for control, she fixed her eyes on one of his fingers. By the way he was flexing it, she knew he was trying to hold on to reason. Dammit! So was she. She spoke with even emphasis on each word. "You said you trusted me to tell you when I was ready. I know this looks like something other than what it is. You must be curious—"

He interrupted her with one terse word. "Curious?"

"Drew, you're making this difficult when it doesn't have to be. I told you, I was taking care of—"

She was cut off again, but this time by the appearance of a car angling halfway into Mrs. Brody's driveway. "I can't believe this is happening," she muttered.

Harold, the gatehouse guard, jumped out of the vehicle. "Don't anyone move," he shouted.

"Harold?" Jill shaded her eyes from the head-lights' beam. "Harold, what are you doing down here?"

"Miss Stuart, are you okay? Is that man hurting you?"

"What? Oh, for heaven's sake. No. This is Ralph Webster's nephew, Drew."

The gate guard moved across the lawn to where she and Drew were standing. Giving Drew a thorough looking-over, he stepped back and tipped his hat. "Then everything's okay? No other suspicious activity going down here?"

"Of course not, Harold. What made you come here?"

"Someone called the gatehouse and said there might be a burglary in progress at Mrs. Brody's place."

Jill pursed her lips, leveling a lethal look toward Drew. "Who called you, Harold?"

"I called him," Ralph said, walking up to the threesome. "What's going on? Is Barbara back?"

"No, she's not," Jill said. "She called me and said her group would be arriving tomorrow. The bus broke down."

Ralph began nodding, then stopped, shifting his gaze between Drew and Jill. "So what's going on?"

Three sets of male eyes turned, as if on cue, to Jill. "Uh, that's simple. Barbara thought . . .

she might have . . . left her stove on. She asked me to check for her." Not the most original excuse, she knew, but certainly an acceptable one. She watched the three men for their reactions.

Harold spoke first. "Happens all the time."

"'Evening, Ralph. Jill. Everything okay?" asked a voice from across the street.

"Everything's fine," Jill answered.

Everything wasn't fine. Several more people were walking across their lawns toward Barbara Brody's front yard, and all were asking questions Jill couldn't answer fast enough.

"What's going on?"

"Is Barbara all right? We haven't seen her in a few days."

"Has Max gotten loose again? I thought he was in the kennel."

Choosing to speak to the residents first, Jill ignored a second car pulling up to the curb. "Please, everyone, calm down. Barbara's fine. There's been no accident, just a misunderstanding by some well-meaning people." Like a well-entrenched reflex, she sought out Drew for confirmation. More people were gathering on the lawn as her stare locked into his. *Tell them it's true, Drew. Back me up.* Rubbing his mouth, he appeared to be considering her unspoken plea. Her stomach clenched like a cold fist when he looked at his uncle. No, this couldn't be happening. But it was. She sensed him withdrawing from her. *You said you trusted me*, she wanted to shout. *You said you'd be here for me.*

When Drew began a private conversation with his uncle, she couldn't stop her hands from shaking. She continued staring at Drew, desperately attempting to will him to be patient with her. His response was a stony look that demanded answers.

"Miss Stuart, what is going on here?" asked an insistent voice at the back of the crowd. The voice got closer. "Miss Stuart, did you hear me?"

The voice was vaguely familiar, but at the moment she wasn't interested in putting a name to it. She didn't have to, because Harold did it for her.

Harold pushed back his uniform cap and nodded. "Mr. Merriweather. Good evening, sir."

Several people stood aside as a grim-faced Mr. Merriweather walked to the center of the small crowd and nodded. "Will someone tell me what's going on?"

Drew was still far from satisfied with the way she'd been treating him, but one thing had remained constant. He loved Jill. He had tried hardening his heart, but her wrenching look of vulnerability cracked it wide open. His need to rescue her rose up inside him, pushing aside every suspicion and misgiving.

"Mr. Merriweather," he said, extending his hand. "I'm Drew Webster of Webster's Landscaping and Gardening Services. I've been in touch with your Nashville office about the Breezy Palms site." He didn't miss Jill's mouth dropping open or her brows kinking with that bit of news.

Mr. Merriweather shook his hand. "Oh, yes." He took a step forward as the crowd began to break up and move away. "Webster."

"Perhaps Miss Stuart will allow me to apologize for this impromptu block party I've created." Drew turned to Jill. He wouldn't have been surprised if he'd seen a return look of panic, or even amazement, but he was wrong on both possibilities. What he did see almost broke his heart. Indifference. No, that was wrong. He looked closer. Losing control as her world crumbled around her had her speechless and dazed.

"The owner of this house is out of town. She called Miss Stuart and asked her to see if her stove had been left on. In the dark and from my uncle's house, I somehow mistook her for a burglar. My error. And as for the crowd," he said, "I've never seen a better support system than the one here at Cinnamon Key. Miss Stuart has a way of keeping the residents caring and involved in the community. She's a distinct asset to your company, Mr. Merriweather."

Jill's bottom lip trembled with the beginning of a grateful smile. He looked away. Saving her butt was one thing, but pretending there wasn't a serious problem between them was another. "Her commitment to this community comes first for her."

Mr. Merriweather mulled over Drew's explanation as Ralph and most of the neighbors began returning to their homes. "Well, Miss Stuart, was it on?"

"On, Mr. Merriweather?"

"The lady's stove."

"No, sir. Mrs. Brody was mistaken." She coughed politely. "Forgive me if I appear stunned, but you usually visit during working hours."

"I left a message on your office answering machine earlier today. Is there something wrong with your machine?"

She felt the tension returning to her body. Just when she thought she was going to make it through this, another crisis threatened her. "No, sir. Today was my day off. I'm sorry, I usually check my machine whenever I'm away from the office." She glanced at Drew. "I . . . didn't get around to that today."

Pursing his lips, Mr. Merriweather's glance bounced between Jill and Drew. "I've no problem with that. Most of your work is resale, and with the high level of satisfaction among these residents, those transactions have been few and far between. You deserve your days off." He smiled knowingly. "I'm sure Mr. Webster agrees."

"Yes, I do."

"I'll be over for those files tomorrow afternoon, Miss Stuart. In case your answering machine doesn't happen to be working, I'll need all we've got on grounds maintenance. Water bills, lawn-care contracts, that sort of thing."

"I'll have them ready."

Drew extended his hand. "I'm looking forward to our meeting day after tomorrow."

"So am I," Mr. Merriweather said, shaking Drew's hand. "Breezy Palms at three in the builder's trailer."

As Mr. Merriweather headed for his car, Jill continued looking at Drew. She'd never been more strongly tempted to explain the promise she'd made to Barbara, but deep down she knew she couldn't. Over the years she'd developed a moral code centered around integrity. Not once, through all the crises in her life, had that code failed her. Even now, when she desperately wanted to spill it all, she knew she'd be abandoning the high point of her character to smooth over one rough moment with Drew. She had to believe he cared enough to understand and that this horrible episode would only make them stronger. She had to believe that. Rubbing her palms together, she quietly whispered, "Thank you."

Sighing impatiently, Drew jammed his fists on his hips and turned his face away. She kept on looking at him. If only the rigid line of his shoulders could soften and meld around her in a forgiving embrace. She pulled in an extra breath and said a silent prayer. His silhouette remained unyielding as the steely tension between them continued, worse than any angry outburst. She couldn't remember ever feeling this anxious. Locking her fingers together in a tight ball, she held them to her chest. "Why didn't you tell me you've been negotiating with him for the Breezy Palms landscaping contract?" When he didn't answer, what little control she had left began slipping away with nervous laughter. "Were you going to surprise me?"

Lifting one hand, he massaged his temple. "Look, I don't want to talk about that right now."

Tears pricked at her eyes. "Why not?" *Why not talk about the things that spell out a future for us? Why not reassure me that I have a reason for the hope I've been harboring in my heart?*

"Why not?" he repeated incredulously. "You'd like to skip over the last fifteen minutes, wouldn't you?"

She threw herself at his mercy with a weak "Yes."

"Well, I can't skip over this," he said, pointing to Barbara Brody's front door. "When something this questionable is going on, and you can't or won't tell me, I can't . . . I won't pretend it doesn't mean anything."

His piercing stare penetrated the darkness between them, sinking into the most tender place inside her. Then he let her hear it from his heart. "A left-on stove, for godsake? What the *hell* do you take me for?" Grabbing her by the shoulders, he drew her up against him. "Tell me, dammit."

His touch brought her to her senses. Banded to his body, she absorbed his power and his passion, making them her own. And then she took the plunge, a free-fall into the unknown. "I take you for what you are," she whispered fiercely. "A passionate, caring man who is being asked to believe in me. To hold off judgment." She reached up, bringing his face closer to hers. "Let me finish what I began. Just—"

With a throaty growl his lips claimed hers, silencing her with ravenous kisses. The kisses went on, chaotic couplings of tongues and moans and ragged breath. He reached to cup her buttocks, pulling her hard against the length of him. She was drowning in desire, heavy with need of his intimate touch. Straining closer, she rubbed her hips against his arousal. "You'll understand. I know you'll understand."

Suddenly he broke the kiss, dragging his face away from hers. As he set her away from him, she felt his arms shaking until the moment he let go. He held up his hand when she began to speak. "No," he said, trying to control his breathing. "Call me when this insanity is over." He turned and walked away, taking half her soul with him.

TEN

He thought another site assessment of Breezy Palms would take his mind off Jill. Standing in the middle of the luxury development, he realized he was wrong. His need to make sense out of the previous night's mess was proving too distracting for him. Throwing his briefcase in the back of his car, he got in and headed for the river road and Lazy Days Boat Rentals.

He pulled into the parking lot, turned off the ignition, and stared out at the sun-dappled water. His unanswered questions and his fears fell away as he drifted back to the day before and Jill. Nothing had bothered them then except birdsong and river sounds, and they had laughed at those things.

Away from uncertain realities, with her arms and legs twined around him, they had drawn out

their pleasure with whispered requests and leisurely responses. The world had been a giving and
forgiving place twenty-four hours earlier. Were
moments like those gone forever? He slammed
his fists on the steering wheel. Why the hell
hadn't he asked her to marry him? Maybe then
she would have told him she needed money. He
would have given it to her. Given her his damn
checkbook, if it would have stopped her from . . .
robbing a white-haired widow blind. *No!* He
pounded the steering wheel again. He had to
be wrong. How could so loving and caring a
person as Jill be stealing from one of her beloved
residents? How could a woman who shared her
sweet, dark passion with him have a conniving
side of this magnitude?

Resting his chin on the back of his hands,
he stared out at a willow tree. The one question
that continued to plague him returned. The one
question that robbed him of sleep during the
night, prevented a civil conversation with his
uncle at breakfast, and ruined his concentration
when he tried to work would not go away. What
had Jill put in her pocket as she left Barbara's?
Something as easily explainable as her wallet?
Or a key case? Or . . . something, anything, that
wasn't Barbara Brody's.

Was it possible his eyes were playing tricks
on him, and she hadn't put anything into her

pocket except her hand? He leaned his head on the headrest and squeezed the steering wheel. What had stopped him from pulling it out of her pocket? Why was he torturing himself? Even Barbara Brody appeared complacent about her losses. Was the older woman under Jill's spell? Was he? None of it made sense.

Once again he'd come to a dead end. Only this time his thoughts detoured back to the river and a moment when Jill's blue-green eyes had looked up into his. The memory of her wide-eyed, love-filled gaze struck him with the force of a velvet-gloved fist. Suddenly, totally and overwhelmingly, he knew he'd made a terrible mistake. Those eyes were not the eyes of a criminal. He laughed out loud at himself.

His uncle had been right about him all along. Drew still loved a good mystery, and although this one hadn't been solved, he knew in his bones that Jill was not the villain. He'd stupidly allowed a poorly lit glimpse of nothing and his energetic imagination to practically ruin their lives.

"Jerk," he said to himself as he started his car and backed out of the parking lot. Feeling sheepishly apprehensive about facing her, he wondered what she would say. She certainly had every reason to kick him out on his ear and toss his apology out after him. Making a right turn out of the parking lot, he drove east on the river road toward Cinnamon Key. Sacrificing another minute in the limbo he'd created would be wasting time away from Jill.

The first thing he was going to do after apologizing was ask her to marry him. He turned on the radio and stepped on the gas pedal. During the short ride to the crossroads at Macomber, he boosted his spirits further by deciding a full-carat, pear-shaped solitaire would look beautiful on her left hand. He had a ton of things to ask her. Had she ever thought about living at Breezy Palms? Some of the floor plans were spectacular, and he knew of one house situated on the far side of the lake that he wanted to show her.

He was making good time on the empty river road, catching the green light and taking the corner smoothly at Macomber. Glancing at the row of storefronts, he hit the brakes as someone removed the velvet glove and punched him hard in his solar plexus. His eyes locked onto Dilby's Pawnshop and Jill. She was standing outside, opening a small, rectangular box. As the early-morning sun gleamed off the stones inside the box, he felt his heart plummeting to his stomach.

Jill felt like an actress in an old-fashioned musical about to burst into song. Mr. Dilby had given her more money than Barbara had predicted. That would have been reason enough to celebrate. Then she'd delivered the requested files to Mr. Merriweather, and he'd asked if she was interested in managing a three-person staff at the new office in Breezy Palms. With fewer hours and a higher salary offered, Jill accepted the offer immediately. To top things off, she'd just delivered the money for the diamond pendant to Barbara. The grateful look on Barbara's face was worth every inconvenient moment over the last few weeks. Well, almost worth that, Jill amended, thinking of Drew. At least Drew was in Florida, and now that she'd finally seen Barbara through the last of this pawning business, she was feeling aggressively optimistic about the final outcome when she would be free to reveal the truth to him. She laughed quietly at her choice of words. Aggressively optimistic. Why not?

After parking behind her building at 21 Cinnamon Circle, she got out, tucked her purse under her arm, and headed for her apartment. The hanging basket of red impatiens was twisting in the breeze under the overhang. She reached up to pull off one perfect flower, then twirled it between her fingertips as she walked on. Today was going to be exceptional, she thought, as she headed around the corner. She stopped dead at the sight in front of her.

Drew was sitting at the bottom of the stairs, resting his elbows on his knees, his fingers laced tightly together. At the moment of her arrival he lifted his face toward her. His expression was without emotion.

"Drew? What's wrong?" The flower fell from her fingers when she went to him with mounting concern. "You look as if you lost your best friend," she said, fearing something much worse. When he didn't answer, she knelt down and took his hands in hers. "Tell me. Is it your uncle?"

"No."

Watching him carefully, she noticed his guarded smile only affected the bottom half of his face. Whatever was weighing on his mind had sapped his energy. Her heart warmed at her next thought. After their parting the night before, coming back to her must be difficult for him. She took his hand and kissed it. None of that painful separating mattered to her now, because he was there. He hadn't waited for her to contact him, he'd come to her, and that was the most important thing.

"Where have you been?" he asked quietly, pulling back his hand.

"Just running some errands," she said, readjusting the purse under her arm. "I had some business on the other side of the causeway, and now that I've taken care of it, I feel marvelous. Funny how getting a little chore out of the way can make your day." He wasn't amused. In fact, his eyes had taken on a flat focus that didn't include her. She leaned down and kissed him on the cheek. Her breath caught in her throat as he flinched. She was pushing him, and she shouldn't. Not with his male ego in tatters around his feet. "I know you didn't come here to hear about my chores. I suspect you'd like to talk about last night. Would you like to come upstairs?"

He remained silent so long, she said his name again. "Drew? I'm awfully glad you—"

"I heard you." He stood up, finally focusing in on her face. "I can't come up. There are some things I have to take care of this afternoon." He looked over her shoulder as he spoke. "Will you come to my uncle's house tonight? Eight o'clock."

"Yes. Are you sure you're okay?" She reached for his arm, but he'd already stepped onto the crushed-shell path.

"I'll see you tonight."

She watched him walk away, putting yards between them in a matter of seconds. That distance didn't frighten her as much as the emotional distance he'd put between them seconds before. A dozen fears swamped her mind. Was he going to tell her he'd made a mistake and was not moving to Florida after all? Did he have a lover in New Jersey he'd suddenly realized he wanted more than her? Surely, he hadn't conjured up another terrible explanation of her secret promise to Barbara, or he would have told her. No, this had to be much worse. This had to be about their relationship.

Her last desperate thought buckled her knees, bringing her bottom in contact with a lower step. She hugged her purse to her breast and shivered with the revelation. She was going to lose him.

At eight o'clock she found herself staring at Ralph Webster's front door. Fighting the desire to turn around and run, she smoothed the front of her flowered skirt, then tugged at the pink linen vest. Retreating at this point would only prolong the inevitable—whatever it was. Shaking her head, she tried with everything in her heart to see beyond this night. She had always been a survivor, she reminded herself. Maybe, just maybe, she wasn't facing the end of the world. She raised her fist to knock when she heard laughter on the other side of the door. Before she could lower her hand, the door swung open.

"Jill. What a surprise," Ralph said, moving

aside to wave her in. "Barbara and I were getting ready to go over to the clubhouse for the Jazz Jam. Would you like to come with us?"

"No, thank you," she said, stepping inside and greeting Barbara with a kiss on the cheek. Barbara had been laughing, and her eyes were shining with merriment.

"Jill, you look upset. What's the matter?"

She gave Barbara's hand an extra squeeze but turned to Ralph when she spoke. "Drew asked me to come by."

"Drew asked you? That's strange." Frowning, Ralph rubbed his chin. "He didn't say anything to me. As a matter of fact, I haven't seen him all day."

Jill's stomach flip-flopped. Was this day's worth of agony about to end in one more painful revelation? "Did he go back to New Jersey?" she asked softly.

Ralph gave her a curious look. "Why would he do that?" he asked, as he reached for the door to close it.

"That was a harebrained question, wasn't it?" she agreed nervously.

"Yes, it was," Drew said, pushing the door open and walking in. The energy in his smoky topaz gaze stole the breath from her body. "I just moved down here. What possible reason would I have to leave this quickly, Jill?"

Drew's expression didn't change, and the speculative silence rolled on. She wondered vaguely if the sudden constriction in her chest and the accompanying queasiness was how a heart attack started.

"Well," Ralph said, guiding Barbara around the younger couple, "if you two will excuse us, we don't want to be late."

Drew pushed the door shut as Ralph reached for the handle. "This is more important, Uncle. We all need to have a talk."

"About what?" Jill asked. Drew's tone hadn't given her a clue, and that fact took her beyond queasy to light-headed.

Drew looked at all three of them. "Maybe we'd better go into the living room and sit down."

"Is this going to take long? Barbara and I wanted to hear this singer who's come all the way over from Fort Lauderdale. We've been looking forward to tonight for weeks."

"Believe me, I want this over as quickly as you," Drew said, leading them all past the kitchen door and into the living room.

Barbara flinched. "Oh, dear. Max heard us." An indignant growl accompanied by a scratching sound continued from the other side of the kitchen door. "I hope he's not marking up the door."

"If you'll take a seat, I want a word with Jill before I go on with this." Drew took Jill by the wrist and pulled her close. "This isn't how I wanted to end it, but after this morning you left me no other choice."

"This morning? What happened this morning?" With his arm locked around her waist, his determination was as frightening as it was provocative. One second she wanted to lean into him and cry, and the next she wanted to run so far, even her memories couldn't find her.

He shook his head with disbelief, then lowered his mouth close to her ear. "Boy, you're not going to give me an inch on this, are you?" he asked in a conspiratorial whisper.

The feel of him hard against her was as tempting as ever. When they were close, he was usually whispering love words. This was no tender entreaty. Tensing, she jerked her head away from the familiar warmth of his breath. "Why do Ralph and Barbara have to be here when you do this?" she whispered, willing him to see the desperation in her eyes.

"Because I want this finished tonight, and bringing everything out in the open is the only way I know to handle it. You ought to know my style by now."

Images swept through her consciousness. Brash male images of Drew. Her mouth opened wider with each succeeding picture. Drew that first morning in her office telling her he knew she was trying to get rid of him...asking her who kissed her the way he did...chopping through the flower stalks...stacking his foil-wrapped "perfectly clear intentions" on her dresser...making love in the gazebo and on the riverbank. The list went on, and the message was the same every time. When Drew decided on action, there was no stopping him. "What are you going to do?"

He released her. "Don't worry, I'm not the theatrical type. I hate all of this, and I'm not going to draw it out," he said, setting his briefcase on the bar and unsnapping the locks.

She looked over at Ralph and Barbara sitting on the couch. Ralph looked impatient with the proceedings. Barbara looked close to a state of panic. "Drew, I insist you tell me what you're going to do," Jill said.

"What I have to do to end this and get on with our lives. I'm here for you and for me." He lowered his head, whispering fiercely. "I can't understand why you couldn't come to me if you needed money."

Jill's head snapped up in shock. This meeting wasn't to be about moving back to New Jersey or reconnecting with an old lover. This was about what it had always been about. His unrelenting investigation over the burglaries that never were.

Ralph spoke up from across the room "Andy," he said sharply, tapping his watch, "this had better be good, because that Jazz Jam is starting in five minutes."

Stepping up his pawing on the door, Max's growl had taken on a serious tone. The swinging door creaked on its hinges.

Barbara started up from the couch. "Maybe I ought to take Max for a walk while you settle this."

"Please don't, Barbara," Drew said. "You're needed here. This concerns all of us."

Jill took a firm hold of Drew's elbow and attempted to turn him away from the sofa. "Don't do this, please. All I'm asking is a few more days."

"You've been asking me for more time all along, but it ran out about ten o'clock this morning, Jill. I saw you going into Dilby's," he said, pulling a paper from his briefcase and handing it to Jill. He gave her shoulder a gentle squeeze. "Be strong. I'll get you through this if it takes every cent I've got. Just tell the truth. Tell them why you did it. Maybe we can work something out with Barbara."

One glance at the letterhead, and the world as she knew it shifted on its axis, throwing everything, including her emotions, into a new orbit. "How did you get this?" she asked angrily.

"Get what?" Ralph asked. "What is going on?"

Ignoring his uncle, Drew answered Jill instead. "I convinced your Mr. Dilby that you were my wife, and that this," he said, bringing out the jewel case, "was your mother's. He allowed me to buy it back for you." Drew shrugged. "He says he deals with ladies in financial trouble quite a lot."

"Andy," Barbara said through nervous laughter, "you've got our Jill white as a ghost. Why are you upsetting her like this?" Max heard his owner's voice and began throwing his body against the kitchen door, distracting everyone's attention.

"Now you've really got the dog upset," Ralph said, getting up and crossing the room. Barbara followed him. "What's going on? What have you got here?" Ralph took the diamond pendant from his nephew. "Look at this, Barbara. Didn't you wear one like it to the dinner dance last month?"

When Barbara saw the pendant, she gave a strangled cry through the flattened fingers against her lips. At that same moment Max managed a successful charge against the door, then shot through the opening. As the little white dog tumbled down the two steps into the living room, Barbara started crying. Undaunted, he righted himself, lunged at Drew, and took a firm bite of his pant leg.

"Oh, Jill, I can't believe it's come to this."

Looking down at his ankle, Drew muttered, "Neither can I."

"Come to what?" Ralph asked. "Will someone tell me what's going on?"

Drew took a deep breath and held it as he nodded for Jill to speak. He let it out quickly when she slapped him on the arm.

"How could you be so insensitive? Can't you see how upset you've made Barbara?"

Ralph was waving his arms. "What is going on?"

Drew looked at Jill. "I've discovered the burglar."

"Burglar? I thought we'd settled that weeks ago," Ralph said.

"N-no . . . weee . . . d-didn't," Barbara said before a fit of sobbing. She put her arms around Jill. "Jill, I'm s-so s-sorry to put you through this."

"You're sorry?" Drew asked. "What do you have to be sorry about, Barbara?"

Jill leveled a lethal look at him. "You are the most impatient man I've ever met. There, there, Barbara. You don't have to answer him."

Barbara lifted her head and sniffed. "I want to, Jill. I've caused enough trouble already with my foolish pride. Andy? Ralph? I have a confession to make."

"You have a confession to make?" Drew asked. Baffled, he looked at Jill.

"Jill accidentally discovered me pawning some of my possessions, and I made her promise to keep it a secret. You see, Dr. Brody had developed a gambling problem, and by the time he died, all that was left were my CD's. I know I could have cashed them in early, but I've done my banking at the same place for years. I'm a proud woman and I couldn't stand the thought that someone there might figure out what a mess Raymond had left me in. I can't imagine anything more humiliating than suffering pitying stares. And people gossip. It would have been a matter of time before my neighbors in Cinnamon Key found out." She looked down at Max, who had detached himself from Drew's pant leg and was sitting on her foot. "We almost made it, didn't we, Jill?"

"Almost."

"Will you ever forgive me for causing you so much trouble?"

"You don't have to ask my forgiveness, Barbara. I chose to keep your secret because I understand how frightening it feels to be on the verge of poverty. I lived most of my life that way. And, anyway, how could I say no to you? You were the one who asked Dr. Brody to write that wonderful letter for Peter's medical school application. Because of that recommendation, he got into a fine school."

"None of this had to happen if you'd told me you were having trouble. I'm your friend too. Why didn't you talk to me, Barbara?" Ralph asked.

The older woman turned to Ralph, wiping away her tears with her fingers. He handed her his handkerchief. "Mostly because I was embarrassed and ashamed. After I started going to Dilby's, though, I have to admit, I started feeling proud of myself." She dabbed her eyes, then gestured with the white cloth. "I mean, I never had to take care of myself before, and it was kind of an adventure."

"I'm terribly sorry to have upset you, Barbara. Please accept my apologies," Drew said.

"Of course I do, Andy." She shook her finger at Drew. "You did make things a tad more challenging, but that only made me see that although I could accomplish this alone, I didn't have to." She smiled at Jill.

Ralph put his arm around Barbara and shook his head with admiration. "A pawnshop. That was a . . . clever choice."

Barbara crumpled the handkerchief under her chin and attempted a crooked smile. "You think so?"

"Absolutely." He turned to Drew and Jill. "Don't you two agree?"

They nodded, both stunned in their own way by the turn of events.

"Jill was wonderful all the way through this. She did have her serious doubts when I told her about Hector."

The two men's eyes met, then turned toward the older woman. "Hector?" they both asked at once.

"Dr. Brody's bookie," said Jill.

"I paid him off a couple of hours ago," added Barbara. She muffled a relieved giggle behind the handkerchief. "Now I don't have to worry about my kneecaps."

"*Kneecaps?*" Drew and Ralph asked at the same moment.

"They're fine," she insisted, flexing her knees. "See?"

Ralph slipped his arms around her shoulders. "Lord, Barbara, you're one of the bravest women I've ever known."

A lump began forming in Jill's throat as she watched Barbara staring up at the older man.

"Really?" Barbara whispered.

His broad smile was his answer. "Would you

mind skipping the Jazz Jam? I think I'd like to go for a walk along the beach," he said, leading Barbara toward the door.

"I'd love to, Ralph."

"Would you two look after Max?" she asked Jill and Drew. Before either could respond, Ralph was closing the door behind them. A second later he opened it long enough to say, "Don't wait up for me, Drew."

The room was quiet except for an occasional whine from Max. Jill stepped into the foyer and picked up the dog. Cuddling Max, she kept her back toward Drew. Painful questions lingered to taunt her. Until they were answered, she couldn't, wouldn't, face him.

"Did you follow me to Dilby's?"

"No, I was driving by on my way back from Breezy Palms. Are you going to let me apol—"

"Have you called the police?"

"Jill, I wouldn't have let it come to that."

She heard him shuffling through his briefcase and then the distinct sound of leather slapping leather.

"I brought my checkbook. I was prepared to write her a check for everything you'd . . . stolen." He cleared his throat. "What I'd thought you'd stolen. I didn't want to press Dilby for a list, in case he'd become suspicious and tip you off." He snorted a laugh.

She wasn't letting him off that easily. "And what if Barbara decided to press charges? Had you thought about that?"

"Yes, I did," he said, reaching into his briefcase again. "I bought two tickets to Paris. For us." He thought he saw her start with that information. Instead of turning around to face him, she calmly pushed open the kitchen door and slid Max into the kitchen. Closing it behind the dog, she headed down the hall.

"Did you hear what I said? I was going to take you out of the country if I had to," he said, waving the tickets after her as he followed her.

"I heard you. Just one more question, Drew," she said, pressing her palms against his bedroom door. "What reason did you think I had for stealing?"

"What else? To pay your brother's tuition," he said, shoving the tickets into his pocket.

That was the only answer she wanted to hear. The only answer she could have accepted from him. Her sigh was close to a moan as she dropped her forehead against the door.

He started to reach for her but stopped himself before he touched her. For the first time he was genuinely afraid of the outcome. Afraid her fragile feelings were about to disintegrate into contempt for him. Measuring his words, he spoke quietly. "Jill, try to understand. I only suspected you last night when I saw you at Barbara's with the jewelry case in your hand, and then, when I accidentally spotted you going into Dilby's with it this morning. . . . Can you see what brought me to this?"

Jill opened his door, and he followed her in. She ought to be saying something. Shouting something. Crying.

"I was angry with you, Jill. I thought we had something very special between us. I couldn't understand why you didn't ask me for help. Hell, I came right out and offered you the money." His voice was suddenly indignant again. "Why didn't you tell me about Barbara's situation?"

Folding her arms across her midriff, she turned, offering a profile of her jutting chin and upturned nose. "There were several good reasons. First," she began, pulling one hand from beneath a breast and stabbing the air with her index finger, "I promised her I wouldn't tell. Second," she continued, flipping another finger from her fist, "you'd made the point that both you and Ralph had had trouble with money-hungry women in your pasts. And third," she said, wagging three fingers at him, "I wanted to know you had faith in me."

"I wanted the same thing."

Pressing her hands to her chest, she turned to face him with raging frustration. "But all I was

asking for was time to take care of the problem."

"And all I wanted was to take care of you."
His own voice dropped to a whisper. "Jill, I'm
so sorry I hurt you."

"And I'm sorry I put you through all this."

Their voices blended with one heartfelt
request. "Forgive me?"

"I love you, Jill."

Her lips parted with the impact of his words.
Her heart was hammering. "I love you too," she
whispered, a smile tugging at her lips.

"Marry me, Jill."

Tears were choking her, and, reaching out to
him, she could only nod. They came together in
a tangle of arms and mouths and broken sighs.
Swaying in his embrace, she pressed her face
against his neck.

"Let me hear you say it," he said, molding
her soft curves against his distinctive masculine
length. Before she could speak, he slanted his
mouth over hers for one more kiss. Then another, and another after that.

"Yes," she finally managed, through a love-
storm of kisses.

When he finally lifted his head, he pulled in a
deep, steadying breath. His hair was falling over
his forehead, enhancing the roguish light in his
eyes. She lifted the hair from his brow and kissed

him there. "Oh, Drew, were you really going to take me to Paris?"

He pulled the tickets from his pocket and leaned away from her enough to tuck the red envelopes between them. She caught them when they began to slip.

"I still want to take you there. On our honeymoon," he said, drinking in her delight and making it his own. The magic of the moment lingered until he suddenly remembered the ring. He'd left it in his briefcase. "I'll be right back," he said, turning toward the door.

Dropping the tickets on the table, she caught his hand and pulled him back. "Whatever it is, it can wait. I'm not through with you yet."

He looked her over from head to toe. His surprised smile turned to playful interest when she pushed him down on the edge of his bed.

"I should have suspected this when you led me to my own bedroom," he said, cupping her buttocks and pulling her closer. He nuzzled her navel through her clothing, then began unbuttoning her blouse. "What's your problem, gorgeous?"

"Nothing I can't handle," she said, shoving her fingers through his hair. "Remember? I take care of all the problems at Cinnamon Key."

She was kissing him again, and, overwhelmed with happiness, he couldn't stop laughing. "I . . . just want to . . . know how . . .

you're going to . . . take care of me . . . wearing all these clothes."

Her kisses ended in a throaty giggle and then a suggestive sigh. "I wore a skirt, didn't I?" she said, right before tumbling him back on the bed.

"Yes, you did, but tonight I want to feel all of you over all of me." As he drew her onto her side, something about her smile squeezed at his heart, reminding him of what he'd put her through. He wanted to experience the total joy of this moment, but remnants of well-deserved guilt had come back. Bowing his head, he managed a humble "Oh, Jill."

"Tell me, darling." Taking his hand, she pressed it against her cheek. "What is it?"

He waited for the lump to ease in his throat before he looked up. "I put you through so much hell."

"I didn't make it so easy for you either," she said, her blond brow furrowing with emotion. "We did the best we could."

"I never stopped loving you, Jill. No matter what things looked like, I never did."

Her knowing smile grew with glowing intensity. "Then don't stop now," she whispered, leaning into his embrace.

THE EDITOR'S
CORNER

Discover heavenly delights and wicked pleasures with **ANGELS AND OUTLAWS**! In the six terrific books in next month's lineup, you'll thrill to heroes who are saints and sinners, saviors and seducers. Each one of them is the answer to a woman's prayer . . . and the fulfillment of dangerous desire. Give in to the sweet temptation of **ANGELS AND OUTLAWS**—you'll have a devil of a good time!

Sandra Chastain starts things off in a big way with **GABRIEL'S OUTLAW**, LOVESWEPT #672. When he's assigned to ride shotgun and protect a pouch of gold en route to the capitol building during Georgia's Gold Rush Days, Gabriel St. Clair tries to get out of it! He'd be sharing the trip, and *very* close quarters, with Jessie James, the spitfire saloon singer whose family has been feuding with his for years . . . and whose smoky kisses had burned him long ago. Gabe had been her first love, but Jessie lost more than her heart when Gabe left the mountain. Seeing him again awakens wicked longings, and Jessie responds with abandon to the man who has always known how to drive her wild. Sandra combines humor and passion to make **GABRIEL'S OUTLAW** a sure winner.

In **MORE THAN A MISTRESS**, LOVESWEPT #673, Leanne Banks tells the irresistible story of another member of the fascinating Pendleton family. You may remember Carly Pendleton from **THE FAIREST OF THEM ALL**, and Garth Pendleton from **DANCE WITH THE DEVIL**. This time we meet Daniel, a man who is tired of being the dependable big brother, the upstanding citizen, and only wants the woman who has haunted his dreams with visions of passion that he's never known. Determined to hide her slightly shady past, Sara Kingston resists Daniel's invitations, but his gaze warms her everywhere he looks. Fascinated by the recklessness beneath his good-guy smile, she yields to temptation—and finds herself possessed. Look forward to seeing more stories about the Pendleton brothers from Leanne in the future.

Marcia Evanick delivers her own unique outlaw in **MY SPECIAL ANGEL**, LOVESWEPT #674. Owen Prescott thinks he's dreaming as he admires the breathtaking beauty on the huge black horse who arrives just in time to save his neck! Nadia Kandratavich is no fantasy, but a sultry enchantress who brought her entire family of Gypsies to live on her ranch. Nadia knows she has no business yearning for the town's golden boy, but his kisses make her hot, wild, and hungry. When prophecy hints that loving this handsome stranger might cost her what she treasures most, Nadia tries to send him away. Can he make her understand that her secrets don't matter, that a future with his Gypsy princess is all he'll ever want? Shimmering with heartfelt emotion, **MY SPECIAL ANGEL** is Marcia at her finest.

BLACK SATIN, LOVESWEPT #675 is from one of our newest stars, Donna Kauffman. A dark bar might be the right place for Kira Douglass to hire an outlaw, but Cole Sinclair isn't looking for a job—and figures the lady with the diamond eyes needs a lesson in playing with danger. He never thought he'd be anyone's hero, but somehow she breathes life back into his embittered soul. She's offered him anything to recover her stolen dolphin; now she vows to fight his demons, to prove to him that she loves him, scars and all, and always will. Donna works her special magic in this highly sensual romance.

Our next outlaw comes from the talented Ruth Owen in **THE LAST AMERICAN HERO**, LOVESWEPT #676. Luke Tyrell knows trouble when he sees it, but when Sarah Gallagher begs the rugged loner to take the job on her ranch, something stirs inside him and makes him accept. His gaze makes her feel naked, exposed, and shamelessly alive for the first time in her life, but can she ignite the flames she sees burning in this sexy renegade's eyes? Branding her body with his lips, Luke confesses his hunger—but hides his fear. Now Sarah has to show him that the only home she wants is in his arms. Fast-rising star Ruth Owen will warm your heart with this touching love story.

Rounding out this month's lineup is **BODY AND SOUL**, LOVESWEPT #677 by Linda Warren. Though Zeke North acts as if the smoky nightclub is the last place on earth he wants to be, he's really imagining how it would feel to make love to a woman whose hands create such sensual pleasure! Chelsea Connors is a seductive angel whose piano playing could drive a man mad with yearning, but he doesn't want to involve her in his brother's trouble. Her spirit is eager for the music she and Zeke can make together. Chelsea aches to share his fight and to soothe old sorrows. He's never taken anything from anyone before for fear of losing his soul, but Chelsea is determined to hold him by giving a love so deep he'd have no choice but to take it. Linda delivers a sexy romance that burns white-hot with desire.

Happy reading!

With warmest wishes,

Nita Taublib

Nita Taublib

Associate Publisher

P.S. Don't miss the spectacular women's novels coming from Bantam in March: **SILK AND STONE** is the spellbinding, unforgettably romantic new novel from nationally bestselling author Deborah Smith; **LADY DANGEROUS** by highly acclaimed Suzanne Robinson pits two powerful characters against each other for a compelling, wonderfully entertaining romance set in Victorian England; and finally, **SINS OF INNOCENCE** by Jean Stone is a poignant novel of four women with only one thing in common: each gave her baby to a stranger. We'll be giving you a sneak peek at these terrific books in next month's LOVESWEPTs. And immediately following this page, look for a preview of the spectacular women's fiction books from Bantam *available now*!

Don't miss these exciting books by your favorite Bantam authors

On sale in January:

THE BELOVED SCOUNDREL
by Iris Johansen

VIXEN
by Jane Feather

ONE FINE DAY
by Theresa Weir

Nationally bestselling author of
THE MAGNIFICENT ROGUE
and
THE TIGER PRINCE

Winner of *Romantic Times*
"Career Achievement" award

Iris Johansen

THE BELOVED SCOUNDREL

Marianna Sanders realized she could not trust this dark and savagely seductive stranger who had come to spirit her away across the sea. She possessed a secret that could topple an empire, a secret that Jordan Draken was determined to wrest from her. In the eyes of the world the arrogant Duke of Cambaron was her guardian, but they both knew she was to be a prisoner in his sinister plot—and a slave to his exquisite pleasure . . .

"Take off your cloak," he repeated softly as his fingers undid the button at her throat. She shivered as his thumb brushed the sensitive cord of her neck.

"It's not a barrier that can't be overcome." He slid the cloak off her shoulders and threw it on the wing chair by the fire. His gaze moved over the riding habit that was as loose and childlike as the rest of the clothes in her wardrobe. "And neither is that detestable garment. It's merely annoying."

"I intend to be as annoying as possible until you give Alex back to me." She added in exasperation, "This is all nonsense. I don't know what you hope to gain by bringing me here."

"I hope to persuade you to be sensible."

"What you deem sensible. You haven't been able to accomplish that in the last three years."

"Because Gregor took pity on you, and I found his pity a dreadful contagious disease." He stepped forward and untied the ribbon that bound one of her braids. "But I'm over it now. Patience and the milk of human kindness are obviously of no avail. I can't do any worse than I—Stand still. I've always hated these braids." He untied the other braid. "That's better." His fingers combed through her hair. "Much better. I don't want to see it braided again while we're here."

The act was blatantly intimate, and her loosened hair felt heavy and sensual as it lay against her back. He was not touching her with anything but his hands in her hair, but she could feel the heat of his body and smell the familiar scent of leather and clean linen that always clung to him. With every breath she drew she had the odd sensation that he was entering her, pervading her. She hurriedly took a step back and asked, "Where am I to sleep?"

He smiled. "Wherever you wish to sleep." A burgundy-rich sensuality colored his voice.

"Then I wish to sleep in Dorothy's house in Dorchester."

He shook his head. "Not possible." He indicated the staircase. "There are four bedchambers. Choose which one you like. I usually occupy the one at the end of the hall."

She stared at him uncertainly.

"Did you think I was going to force you? I'm sorry to rob you of your first battle, but I have no taste for rape. I'm only furnishing a setting where we'll be close, very close. I'll let Fate and Nature do the rest." He nodded to a door leading off the parlor. "Your workroom. I've furnished it with tools and glass and paint."

"So that I can make you a Window to Heaven?" She smiled scornfully. "What are you going to do? Stand over me with a whip?"

"Whips aren't the thing either. I wanted you to have something to amuse you. I knew you were accustomed to working, and I thought it would please you."

She crossed the parlor and threw open the door to reveal a low-ceilinged room with exposed oak beams. She assumed the dark green velvet drapes covered a window. The room was not at all like her workroom in the tower.

But a long table occupied the center of the room and on that table were glass and tools and paints.

Relief soared through her, alleviating a little of the tension that had plagued her since they had left Cambaron.

Salvation. She could work.

"And you, in turn, will amuse me." He gestured to the large, thronelike high-backed chair in the far corner. "I know you were reluctant three years ago to let me watch you at your craft, but circumstances have changed."

"Nothing has changed." She strode over to the

window and jerked back the curtains to let light pour into the room, then went to the table and examined the tools. "I'll ignore you now, as I would have then."

"You wouldn't have ignored me," he said softly. "If I hadn't been a soft fool, you would have been in my bed before a week had passed. Perhaps that very night."

She whirled on him. "No!"

"Yes."

"You would have forced me?"

"No force would have been necessary."

Heat flooded her cheeks. "I'm not Lady Carlisle or that—I'm not like them."

"No, you're not like them. You're far more alive, and that's where both temptation and pleasure lie. From the beginning you've known what's been between us as well as I have." He looked into her eyes. "You want me as much as I want you."

In the bestselling tradition of Amanda Quick, a spectacular new historical romance from the award-winning

Jane Feather

VIXEN

Chloe Gresham wasn't expecting a warm welcome—after all her new guardian was a total stranger. But when Sir Hugo Lattimer strode into Denholm Manor after a night of carousing and discovered he'd been saddled with an irrepressible and beautiful young ward, the handsome bachelor made it perfectly clear he wanted nothing to do with her. Chloe, however, had ideas of her own. . . .

"Come on, lass." Hugo beckoned. "It's bath time."

Chloe stood her ground, holding on to the back of the chair, regarding Hugo with the deepest suspicion. "I don't want a bath."

"Oh, you're mistaken, lass. You want a bath most urgently." He walked toward her with soft-paced purpose and she backed away.

"What are you going to *do?*"

"Put you under the pump," he said readily, sweeping her easily into his arms.

"But it's freezing!" Chloe squealed.

"It's a warm night," he observed in reassuring

accents that Chloe didn't find in the least reassuring.

"Put me down. I want to go to bed, Hugo!"

"So you shall . . . so you shall. All in good time." He carried her out to the courtyard. "In fact, we'll *both* go to bed very soon."

Chloe stopped wriggling at that. Despite fatigue and the events of the night, she realized she was far from uninterested in what such a statement might promise.

"Why can't we heat some water and have a proper bath," she suggested carefully.

"It would take too long." He set her down beside the pump, maintaining a hold on her arm. "And it would not convince you of the consequences of headstrong, willful behavior. If you dash into the midst of an inferno, you're going to come out like a chimney sweep." Releasing her arm, he pulled the nightgown over her head so she stood naked in the moonlight.

"And chimney sweeps go under the pump," he declared, working the handle.

A jet of cold water hit her body and Chloe howled. He tossed the soap toward her. "Scrub!"

Chloe thought about dashing out of the freezing jet and into the house, but the filth pouring off her body under the vigorous application of the pump convinced her that she had no choice but to endure this punitive bath. She danced furiously for a few moments, trying to warm herself, then bent to pick up the soap and began to scrub in earnest.

Hugo watched her with amusement and rapidly rising desire. The gyrations of her slender body, silvered in the moonlight, would test the oaths of a monk. She was in such a frantic hurry to get the job over and done with that her movements were devoid of either artifice or invitation, which he found even more arousing.

"I hate you!" she yelled, hurling the soap to the ground. "Stop pumping; I'm clean!"

He released the handle, still laughing. "Such an entrancing spectacle, lass."

"I hate you," she repeated through chattering teeth, bending her head as she wrung the water out of the soaked strands.

"No, you don't." He flung the thick towel around her shoulders. "Rarely have I been treated to such an enticing performance." He began to dry her with rough vigor, rubbing life and warmth into her cold, clean skin.

"I didn't mean to be enticing," she grumbled somewhat halfheartedly, since the compliment was pleasing.

"No, that was part of the appeal," he agreed, turning his attentions to the more intimate parts of her anatomy. "But I trust that in the future you'll think twice before you fling yourself into whatever danger presents itself, my headstrong ward."

Chloe knew perfectly well that given the set of circumstances, she would do the same thing, but it seemed hardly politic or necessary to belabor the issue, particularly when he was doing what he was doing. Warmth was seeping through her in little ripples, and, while her skin was still cold, her heated blood flowed swiftly.

Finally, Hugo dropped the towel and wrapped her in the velvet robe. "Run inside now and pour yourself another tot of rum. You can dry your hair at the range. I'm going to clean myself up."

"Oh?" Chloe raised an eyebrow. "I'm sure it would be easier for you if I worked the pump." She turned up her blistered palms. "I've had a good deal of practice already . . . and besides, I'm entitled to my revenge . . . or do I mean *my* pleasure."

Hugo smiled and stripped off his clothes. "Do your worst, then, lass." He faced her, his body fully aroused, his eyes gleaming with challenge and promise.

With a gleeful chuckle she sent a jet of water over him, careful to circumvent that part of his body that most interested her. Hugo was unperturbed by the cold, having enjoyed many baths under the deck pump of one of His Majesty's ships of the line. The secret was to know it was coming.

With the utmost seriousness he washed himself as she continued to work the handle, but deliberately he offered himself to her wide-eyed gaze. She worked the pump with breathless enthusiasm, her tongue peeping from between her lips, her eyes sparkling with anticipation.

"Enough!" Finally, he held up his hands, demanding surcease. "The show's over. Pass me the towel."

Chloe grinned and continued to work the handle for a few more minutes. Hugo leapt out of the stream and grabbed the damp towel. "You're asking for more trouble, young Chloe." He rubbed his hair and abraded his skin.

"Inside with you, unless you want to go under again." He took a menacing step toward her and with a mock scream she ran into the house, but instead of going to the kitchen she went into Hugo's bedroom, diving beneath the sheets.

When he came in five minutes later, she was lying in his bed, the sheet pulled demurely up to her chin, her cornflower eyes filled with the rich sensuality that never failed to overwhelm him.

"Good morning, Sir Hugo." She kicked off the cover, offering her body, naked, translucent in the pearly dawn light.

"Good morning, my ward." He dropped the towel from his loins and came down on the bed beside her.

ONE FINE DAY

Theresa Weir

The bestselling author of *Last Summer* and *Forever*
offers her most poignant and passionate novel yet.

*After too many years of heartache, Molly Bennet had
packed her bags and run away . . . from her memories,
her husband, and the woman she had become. But just
as she found herself on the brink of a brand-new life, an
unexpected tragedy called her home. Now the man who
had always been so much stronger than Molly needs her
in a way she'd never thought possible. . . .*

"If I touch you . . . you won't run, will you?
Please . . . don't run away."

And there it was again. That ragged catch in
his voice.

And there it was again. Her weakening resolve.
Things were so much easier when you knew who
the enemy was. "No," she whispered. "I won't run."

He reached for her. His fingers touched her
arm, skimming across her skin until he grasped
her hand. He pulled her toward him. She took one
hesitant step, then another.

He lifted her hand . . . and he kissed it. He kissed the chewed nails that were her shame, that she thought so unsightly. His lips touched her palm, her knuckles. Then he pulled in a shaky breath and pressed her hand to the side of his face. She could feel his beard stubble. She could feel the heat of his skin.

And even though she tried to harden herself against him, it did no good. There was no anger left in her. Instead, what she felt was a sweet, unbearable sadness. A sadness that was much worse than anger.

And she found herself wanting to comfort him. She had to fight the urge to wrap her arms around him and pull his head to her breast.

Austin had never stirred such ineffable emotions in her. All her life she'd taken care of the people around her. Sammy . . . Amy . . . But Austin had always been so strong, so invincible. He'd never needed anybody. He'd certainly never needed her.

The limb above their heads creaked. Crickets sang from the deep grass near the edge of the yard.

Austin took both of her hands in his. "Remember that time, shortly after we first met?" he asked. "It was dark. I took you to the park . . . and pushed you in the swing. Do you remember?"

At first she didn't, but then she did. "Yes."

They had laughed together that night. But since then their marriage had contained very little laughter. What had happened to them? she wondered. Where had that kind of joy gone? Why had two such ill-suited people ever gotten married in the first place?

Had there ever been any kind of love between them? Had there ever been a time when their marriage hadn't been so bad?

If nothing else, she had to acknowledge the fact that Austin had given her what Jay couldn't—security.

She could also admit that there had been a brief period of time when they'd gone through the motions of being a family. And in the process, they'd almost become one for real. But it had taken only a carelessly spoken word, a look, to shatter that fragile structure.

"And you . . . sat . . . with me," Austin said.

It was true. She'd forgotten that, too, but now she remembered. She'd sat facing him, a lover's position.

She stood in front of him now, her hands in his. Above them, beyond the leaves, beyond the branches, beyond the jet streams, the stratosphere, and the ionosphere, was what Amy would have called a cartoon moon. Its light wasn't an intrusive light, but merely a hello. A comfort, a candle burning in the window. Beneath it, beneath the shelter of leaves, they were wrapped in the indigo velvet of the night.

He pulled her closer, so they were knee to knee. "It was . . . snowing."

Yes. It *had* been snowing. She'd forgotten that too. And now she remembered how strong his arms had been. How safe he'd made her feel with those arms around her.

Maybe she had almost loved him. Maybe she could have grown to love him, if only things had been different . . .

"I made you . . . wear . . . my coat."

He'd wrapped it around her, thick and warm and scented with the cold.

What had happened to those two people? Where had they gone?

She had no idea what made her do what she did next—she'd never initiated anything between them—but she slipped off her sandals, the grass cool and damp under her bare feet. With both hands on the ropes, she stood facing Austin, knee to knee. He gripped her waist to help steady her as she slid her legs on either side of him, her sundress riding up around her thighs.

His hands moved to her bottom, settling her more firmly against him. Then he grasped the rope, his hands just above hers.

"Ready?" he whispered.

He seemed like the old Austin. The Austin she'd forgotten but now remembered. He was strong, confident, his voice so deep it reverberated against her chest. And yet he was a different Austin too. More mature. More aware. And mixed in with those two people was a stranger, someone she didn't know at all.

Was she ready? "Yes."

And don't miss these spectacular
romances from
Bantam Books, on sale in February:

SILK AND STONE
by Deborah Smith
In the compelling tradition of *Blue Willow*,
an enchanting new novel of the heart.

LADY DANGEROUS
by the nationally bestselling author
Suzanne Robinson

SINS OF INNOCENCE
by Jean Stone
A poignant novel of four women with only
one thing in common:
each gave her baby to a stranger.

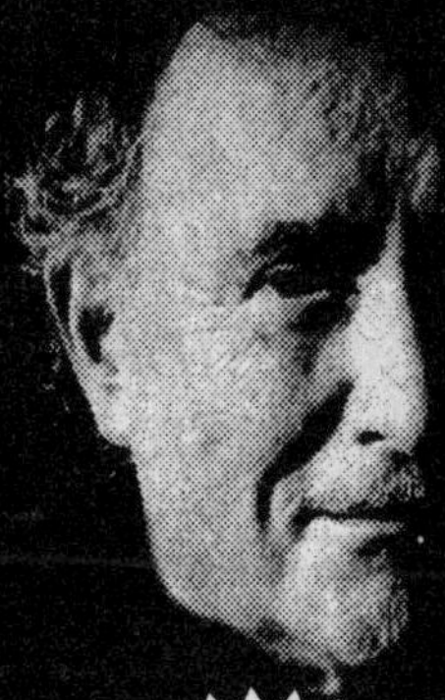

OFFICIAL RULES

To enter the sweepstakes below carefully follow all instructions found elsewhere in this offer.

The **Winners Classic** will award prizes with the following approximate maximum values: 1 Grand Prize: $26,500 (or $25,000 cash alternate); 1 First Prize: $3,000; 5 Second Prizes: $400 each; 35 Third Prizes: $100 each; 1,000 Fourth Prizes: $7.50 each. Total maximum retail value of Winners Classic Sweepstakes is $42,500. Some presentations of this sweepstakes may contain individual entry numbers corresponding to one or more of the aforementioned prize levels. To determine the Winners, individual entry numbers will first be compared with the winning numbers preselected by computer. For winning numbers not returned, prizes will be awarded in random drawings from among all eligible entries received. Prize choices may be offered at various levels. If a winner chooses an automobile prize, all license and registration fees, taxes, destination charges and, other expenses not offered herein are the responsibility of the winner. If a winner chooses a trip, travel must be complete within one year from the time the prize is awarded. Minors must be accompanied by an adult. Travel companion(s) must also sign release of liability. Trips are subject to space and departure availability. Certain black-out dates may apply.

The following applies to the sweepstakes named above:

No purchase necessary. You can also enter the sweepstakes by sending your name and address to: P.O. Box 508, Gibbstown, N.J. 08027. Mail each entry separately. Sweepstakes begins 6/1/93. Entries must be received by 12/30/94. Not responsible for lost, late, damaged, misdirected, illegible or postage due mail. Mechanically reproduced entries are not eligible. All entries become property of the sponsor and will not be returned.

Prize Selection/Validations: Selection of winners will be conducted no later than 5:00 PM on January 28, 1995, by an independent judging organization whose decisions are final. Random drawings will be held at 1211 Avenue of the Americas, New York, N.Y. 10036. Entrants need not be present to win. Odds of winning are determined by total number of entries received. Circulation of this sweepstakes is estimated not to exceed 200 million. All prizes are guaranteed to be awarded and delivered to winners. Winners will be notified by mail and may be required to complete an affidavit of eligibility and release of liability which must be returned within 14 days of date on notification or alternate winners will be selected in a random drawing. Any prize notification letter or any prize returned to a participating sponsor, Bantam Doubleday Dell Publishing Group, Inc., its participating divisions or subsidiaries, or the independent judging organization as undeliverable will be awarded to an alternate winner. Prizes are not transferable. No substitution for prizes except as offered or as may be necessary due to unavailability, in which case a prize of equal or greater value will be awarded. Prizes will be awarded approximately 90 days after the drawing. All taxes are the sole responsibility of the winners. Entry constitutes permission (except where prohibited by law) to use winners' names, hometowns, and likenesses for publicity purposes without further or other compensation. Prizes won by minors will be awarded in the name of parent or legal guardian.

Participation: Sweepstakes open to residents of the United States and Canada, except for the province of Quebec. Sweepstakes sponsored by Bantam Doubleday Dell Publishing Group, Inc., (BDD), 1540 Broadway, New York, NY 10036. Versions of this sweepstakes with different graphics and prize choices will be offered in conjunction with various solicitations or promotions by different subsidiaries and divisions of BDD. Where applicable, winners will have their choice of any prize offered at level won. Employees of BDD, its divisions, subsidiaries, advertising agencies, independent judging organization, and their immediate family members are not eligible.

Canadian residents, in order to win, must first correctly answer a time limited arithmetical skill testing question. Void in Puerto Rico, Quebec and wherever prohibited or restricted by law. Subject to all federal, state, local and provincial laws and regulations. For a list of major prize winners (available after 1/29/95): send a self-addressed, stamped envelope entirely separate from your entry to: Sweepstakes Winners, P.O. Box 517, Gibbstown, NJ 08027. Requests must be received by 12/30/94. DO NOT SEND ANY OTHER CORRESPONDENCE TO THIS P.O. BOX.